SECRET LANDS

The Patricia Lynch Collection

for

everyone on the CBI
Committee

Many thanks for an excellent
Conference, October '98 –

Robert Dunbar

ROBERT DUNBAR

Robert Dunbar lectures in English in the Church of Ireland College of Education, Dublin. He also teaches a course in children's literature at Trinity College and contributes to the M.A. programme in children's literature at St Patrick's College of Education. He has lectured on many aspects of children's literature in Ireland and abroad and is a regular reviewer of children's books for a wide range of newspapers, magazines and radio programmes. He was a founder member and twice president of CLAI (Children's Literature Association of Ireland) and is a member of CBI (Children's Books Ireland). He was chairperson of the Bisto Book of the Year awards committee on three occasions and edited the first fifteen issues of *Children's Books in Ireland*. His anthology *Enchanted Journeys: Fifty Years of Irish Writing for Children*, published by The O'Brien Press, was one of the bestselling Irish children's books of 1997 and won a White Ravens award. He has contributed the entries on Patricia Lynch, P.J. Lynch and W.B. Yeats to the forthcoming *Oxford Companion to Fairy Tales*. He was born in Ballymoney, Co. Antrim, and was Head of English at Rainey Endowed School, Magherafelt, before moving to Dublin in 1980. He has recently been nominated a patron of Children's Books Ireland.

SECRET LANDS

THE WORLD OF PATRICIA LYNCH

EDITED BY
ROBERT DUNBAR

Illustrated by Aileen Johnston

THE O'BRIEN PRESS
DUBLIN

First published 1998 by The O'Brien Press Ltd.
20 Victoria Road, Rathgar, Dublin 6, Ireland.
Tel. +353 1 4923333; Fax. +353 1 4922777
e-mail: books@obrien.ie
website: http://www.obrien.ie

ISBN: 0-86278-575-8

British Library Cataloguing-in-publication Data
Lynch, Patricia, 1894-1972
Secret lands : the Patricia Lynch collection
1.Children's stories, English
I.Title II.Dunbar, Robert
823.912[J]

1 2 3 4 5 6 7 8 9 10
98 99 00 01 02 03 04 05

The O'Brien Press receives
assistance from

The Arts Council
An Chomhairle Ealaíon

Typesetting, layout, design: The O'Brien Press Ltd.
Cover illustration: Aileen Johnston
Cover separations: Lithoset Ltd., Dublin
Printing: Biddles Ltd.

DEDICATION

For all who travel in secret lands

Acknowledgements

I am grateful to a number of people whose help and co-operation have made possible the publication of this anthology: Mai and Eugene Lambert, for a wonderful day in their home, when they shared their memories of Patricia Lynch and their knowledge of her work; the librarians and staff of the National Library of Ireland and of St Patrick's College of Education, for providing access to her earlier and out of print books; Aileen Johnston, whose cover and illustrations have remarkably captured those qualities of her work which I have attempted to capture also in my excerpts; Ide ní Laoghaire and Rachel Pierce, my editors at The O'Brien Press, whose constructive comments have ensured a better book than it would otherwise have been; and, finally, my wife Carole, whose positive and practical encouragement has enabled me to see the project through and remain cheerful in the process.

Contents

BIOGRAPHY OF
PATRICIA LYNCH

Patricia Lynch was born in Cork in 1894. Her father died while she was still very young and she spent her early childhood years travelling, usually with her mother, between Ireland, England, Scotland and Belgium. In Cork she had been exposed, through local shanachies, to the tradition of oral story-telling, which held a lasting fascination for her. She attended a number of schools in the different countries where she travelled. She was at all times an enthusiastic reader and was later to acknowledge the influence on her work of various other children's writers, including E. Nesbit. Her first published writing, when she was in her twenties and living in London, was in the form of journalism. One particular article, entitled 'Scenes from the Rebellion' and written originally for *The Workers' Dreadnought*, a Suffragette newspaper, became famous as one of the first and most graphic eye-witness accounts of the events in Dublin during Easter 1916. In 1922 she married an English writer, R.M. Fox, and soon afterwards they settled in Glasnevin in Dublin. Her earliest children's stories to be published in Ireland appeared first in *The Irish Press* in 1931. It was in this newspaper also that the novel which subsequently appeared in 1934 as *The Turf-Cutter's Donkey* was first published, in serialised form. Between then and 1967, when her last children's novel was published, she wrote some fifty children's books in a variety of genres: these included historical fiction, fantasy and the realistic adventure story. Many of them were illustrated by distinguished artists of the time, including Sean Keating, Harry Kernoff and Jack B. Yeats. Her work was translated into a number of European languages and several of her books were awarded national and international prizes. Following her husband's death in 1969, she moved to Monkstown, Co. Dublin, into the home of her friends, Mai and Eugene Lambert, where she remained until her death in 1972. Her grave is in Glasnevin cemetery.

RECOLLECTIONS OF
PATRICIA LYNCH

Eugene Lambert

In the early 1960s R.M. Fox, theatre critic and journalist, interviewed me at the Olympia Theatre where I was performing my ventriloquist act in a variety show. At the conclusion of the interview he asked me for a photograph of myself and Finnegan, my ventriloquist doll. He gave me his address to send the photograph to him: 39 The Rise, Glasnevin. I said that I would drop it in as it was only a stone's throw from where I lived in Finglas. Next day I brought the photograph to R.M. and to my amazement and delight I was introduced to his wife, Patricia Lynch.

I had known Patricia Lynch through her books since I was a child and to meet her in reality was just marvellous. Patricia was a very slight, frail lady with a slight cockney accent, a twinkle in her eye and an impish sense of humour. Their house was built in 1936 and had remained a time capsule as nothing had been altered since the day the builder left. A small lawn in front of the house had several large conifers which slightly shaded it. Patricia's rare garden was a virtual fairy glen, with elder trees for her famous wine, bluebells, primroses and all sorts of wild flowers. She had a tiny patch which she used to cultivate while sitting on a box; barely breaking the soil with a hand-rake she grew a small crop of strawberries and vegetables.

The front door led into a hall on either side of which was a room; the right hand room was R.M.'s study and on the left was the living-room where Patricia wrote.

A slight musty odour of elderberries, cloves, apples and books permeated the house. Patricia's room was sparsely furnished: an old Chesterfield, two small armchairs, upholstered butter boxes on either side of the fireplace, two small glass cabinets which had been given to her by students at Kevin Street Technical College to hold copies of her books and memorabilia, and an oak writing desk which doubled as a dining table.

R.M.'s study would have seemed a completely chaotic clutter to an outsider, with orange boxes and shoe boxes and rickety shelving. He had his own method of 'filing', yet he could put his hand on any article, manuscript, contract, book or letter without any hesitation.

Both Patricia and Dick (as R.M. was also known) worked at their writing, each in their own room, every day except Wednesday afternoon when they had visitors for tea.

Patricia wrote in long-hand, using recycled paper–this was before it was fashionable. Then Dick would type her work into manuscript form on his old Underwood mechanical typewriter. Patricia even wrote a book in long-hand when she was totally blind with cataracts and

Dick remarked that he had to decipher most of it off the table-cloth. This was before I had met her; by then her cataract operation had been totally successful.

A great friendship grew out of my first meeting with R.M. and Patricia – not only with me but with the whole family.

Our family consisted of my wife Mai and our ten children – seven boys and three girls. Patricia loved birthday parties and we had one a month at least. My own is the fifth and Patricia's the seventh of June so we always celebrated them together. The children got on very well with Patricia and Dick. Dick taught the boys to play chess and we later learned that Patricia used to write excuse notes in Mai's name for some of the boys to present to their teachers. One of the boys said to his teacher: 'You would not have thrown the note away if you had known who really wrote it.'

Patricia and Dick had no family of their own and even though Patricia had written so many wonderful stories for children, she really had very little contact with them. On one occasion, when Mai and I had to go to the RTE studios, Patricia offered to look after the two youngest boys. They were about five and six years of age at the time. We did our day's work in RTE, working on *Murphy agus a Chairde*, and then returned to Patricia's house to collect the two boys.

'I hope the two lads didn't give you any bother, Patricia,' I said.

Patricia replied, 'Sure, they were no trouble at all. They had a lovely day altogether tasting my elderberry wine.'

Sprawled fast asleep on the Chesterfield lay the two boys. We carried them home to our own house and they didn't wake up until the middle of the next day.

One morning Dick rang quite early. 'Could you come down at once?' he said. We thought something had happened to Patricia; she had already had several slight heart attacks. But no: Findlaters had stopped delivering groceries and they had had a regular standing order for years; what should he do? Well, we were already shopping for twelve so two more made no difference. We delivered groceries to them from then on and they were also frequent and delightful dinner guests in our busy home.

After that, we really adopted each other. We went to all sorts of functions together: Cork Film Festival, Listowel Writers' Week, Sligo Yeats Summer School, Belfast PEN. I could go on and on; Patricia would never turn down an opportunity to travel. We also went to the theatre very often as both Patricia and R.M. were avid theatre- and film-goers and never missed an opening night. They were known affectionately in all the theatres as the 'little foxes'.

Patricia was really pleased when RTE decided to make a puppet serial of *Brogeen Follows the Magic Tune,* and so were we. She enjoyed its success and she loved coming to our house to see each episode.

R.M. died at Christmas in 1969. It was a great shock to Patricia. She came to live with us in Monkstown when we moved and she saw the beginning of the Lambert Puppet Theatre. To me and my family it was a great honour to have known her, a kind and gentle person. She will always be with us through her writing.

INTRODUCTION

The Cork in which Patricia Lynch was born and in which she spent her early childhood years provided an environment where the oral and literary tradition of native story-telling was remarkably strong. In her autobiographical *A Story-Teller's Childhood*, published in 1947, she pays particular tribute to a Mrs Hennessy, described as 'a shanachie, one of the real old story-tellers', who was to become a powerful influence on the young child, transmitting to her a treasure hoard of Irish stories and imbuing her with what was to be a life-long fascination with them. When she came to write her fifty or so children's novels, it is not surprising that so many of them evince her indebtedness to childhood memories of story, a comment which applies even to those of her books which set out to be realistic in tone and setting.

The result is a body of work in which the fictional world with which we are presented is a place where reality and fantasy are very closely linked, and where the picture of Ireland which emerges is of a terrain where the possibility of magical experiences lies around every corner. The stories, like those which Ethne Cadogan listens to at the *ceilidhe* in the Widow Rafferty's house in the 1941 novel *Fiddler's Quest*, are invariably 'of strange happenings and enchantments'. The written form in which we read them bears many of the hallmarks of their oral predecessors: the improvisatory air, the fondness for anecdote, the reliance on dialogue and the quickly changing atmosphere and tone.

Significant as the memory of local, oral story-telling was in influencing Patricia Lynch in her choice of theme and in her style of writing, it is not the only signpost to the 'secret lands' of her children's fiction. As with most writers, she was influenced also by the wider literary and social developments of the period in which she lived and wrote. Thus, although she was born too late to be seen as a major player in the movement popularly known as the Irish Literary Revival, it is impossible to separate the recurring themes of her children's books from the aspirations of the revivalists, not least because they too were founded in a long established oral tradition.

The desire of revivalists such as Standish O'Grady and, later, Yeats to restore Ireland's cultural heritage, a restoration which involved a rediscovery of its ancient Gaelic sagas and a recognition of the strength and colour of its folklore, had resulted in an abundance of re-tellings and novelisations of the country's oldest stories. Patricia Lynch would have endorsed these acts of reclamation, as can be seen in subsequent re-tellings of her own, such as *Tales of Irish Enchantment*, published in 1952, and in numerous references throughout her fiction to the personages and events celebrated in the ancient sagas. When Fiona in *Fiona Leaps the Bonfire* (1957) meets Cúchulainn and asks for details of what he did when he was young, he replies, 'So you love hearing stories! Isn't it grand that every day which passes more stories are being lived and dreamed, so that as we grow older our minds grow richer'. The great hero's emphasis on stories being 'lived and dreamed', and as a source of continuing enrichment, fits well with Revival ideals. It is also interesting that in the novel *The Golden Caddy* (1962) one of her characters is reading Standish O'Grady's best known boys' adventure story, *Lost on Du-Corrig*.

While the vibrant indigenous stories which the revivalists sought to recover had this heroic dimension, they had one further important – though perhaps less elevated – characteristic which was to influence much Irish writing for children, Patricia Lynch's included. In its broadest sense, this characteristic lies in the stories' fundamental concern with the supernatural and with the visions and metamorphoses which occur when the supernatural impinges on human affairs. In the children's fiction which derives from these preoccupations, the natural and the possible are deserted for the impossible and the irrational, chiefly in the form of fantastic exaggeration which can be enjoyed only if there is, on the reader's part, a total suspension of disbelief.

Where Patricia Lynch's work of this kind is concerned, it has to be conceded that the quality of her achievement is inconsistent. Many of her full-length fantasy stories are, in effect, fairy tales, witnessing her fondness for employing the structures and motifs of the genre. Her most successful books in this category include *The Grey Goose of Kilnevin* (1939) and *Jinny the Changeling* (1959), both characterised by a Yeatsian sense of longing to recapture a lost childhood, the cry of the heart, as Yeats himself put it, against necessity, although the yearning is undercut in Lynch's case by her sense of humour. Some of her short stories in fairy tale style, such as 'The Shadow Pedlar' and 'The Little Fiddler', rank among her greatest achievements, combining her usual exuberance with a discipline in the telling and with a haunting sense of otherworld atmosphere.

In the introduction to his *Fairy and Folk Tales of the Irish Peasantry* (1888), Yeats had reminded his readers that the fairies 'have only one industrious person amongst them, the lepracaun – the shoemaker'. For Patricia Lynch, it was to be one of these 'industrious' beings, in the form of Brogeen, who provided the protagonist for a sequence of novels in which she featured the adventures of the fairy folk who live in the Fairy Fort of Sheen. The confusing variety of these fairy folk is admirably summed up in *Brogeen Follows the Magic Tune* (1952) as 'leprechauns, cluricauns, phoukas, banshees, glashans and the like'. Several of these characters, including Brogeen himself, appear also in the novels which deal with the resourceful and omniscient Long Ears, the donkey who made his debut in *The Turf-Cutter's Donkey*, first published in book form in 1934. These, like the Brogeen books, are typified by a level of activity which borders on the frenetic and by an emphasis on the kind of transformational magic which ensures a rapidly changing plot-line.

Undeniably, these Brogeen and Long Ears stories have their vivacious moments and occasionally their inventiveness can border on the surreal, reminiscent (at their best) of Lewis Carroll or, to cite a more local parallel, the James Stephens of *The Crock of Gold*. But, as both series came increasingly to be extended, the potential of many of the novels was diminished by their repetitiveness and by their reliance on a form of miraculous intervention lacking in subtlety or sharpness. For the modern reader, there is a danger that the stories' original, simple charm may now seem to be mere whimsy or sentimentality, the literary equivalent, perhaps, of a dated John Hinde postcard view of the Irish landscape.

When Patricia Lynch deals with the reality of that

landscape, as distinct from the fantasy which she sees as one of its inescapable dimensions, she approaches the Ireland of her time in a manner which again, certainly for the modern reader, may create some difficulty in understanding or identification. In her depiction of, essentially, a rural Ireland – only a few of her books have urban settings – she conveys a picture of village and small-town communities where the day to day routine of making a living is alleviated only by the excitement of outings to the fair or to the travelling circus or to the horse races. There may be family quarrels and sibling rivalries and jealousies (sometimes presented with considerable psychological awareness, as in her 1953 novel *Delia Daly of Galloping Green*) but an ultimate amicable resolution is always assured. The virtues of self-help and neighbourly solidarity are endorsed, the values of hearth and home, or hearth and cabin, are celebrated.

The less attractive aspect here, however, is that Lynch's communities tend to be inward-looking and suspicious, attitudes most clearly seen in the way in which she portrays their responses to that group of human beings known generally in the Ireland of her time as 'the tinkers'. They are not always seen as lawless, deceitful villains – some of them, Autolycus-like, are endowed with nothing more dangerous than a romanticised fecklessness – but they are frequently portrayed as objects of fear and mistrust, as in the opening chapter of *The Turf-Cutter's Donkey*. It is usually the older members of the settled communities who demonstrate their prejudices. The young have a more welcoming, less inhibited outlook, as is seen in Tessa Nolan's reaction to Dara MacDara, the 'tinker boy' of the 1955 novel of that title: the contrast between her spontaneous gesture of friendship to the boy and the guarded distance maintained by her teacher is very obvious. But, welcome as these moments of generosity are, they do not quite compensate for an overall view of 'tinkers' which, in less enlightened times than our own, might well have encouraged notions of stereotyping and discrimination.

There is one extremely important aspect of the reality of Patricia Lynch's Ireland which, to her credit, she was not afraid to confront in her children's fiction. The 1940s, 1950s and 1960s were years of large-scale emigration from Ireland, whether temporary or permanent, resulting in family and community break-up and in its accompanying human tragedies. This, clearly, is a theme which struck a sympathetic chord with the novelist. The pattern of separation, journey and (possible) return which is found as a recurring motif in fairy tale and legend is a universal phenomenon, but it has a striking appropriateness in a country where emigration and exile have played such a major part in its history.

Lynch's attraction to the structure of fairy tale thus stood her in very good stead here and allowed her to include numerous poignant scenes of farewell and departure. The chapter 'The Liverpool Boat' from her 1956 novel *The Bookshop on the Quay* provides a good example of this. As Shane walks the Dublin quays in search of his Uncle Tim, he is aware of the almost crazed confusion which emigration brings with it: 'Cries of "Goodbye now!" "We'll see you to the boat!" "Don't forget your old friends!" "Come back with a fortune!" "Mind you write a long letter every week!" were tossed along the quays. Hootings and shouts and splashings rose from the river and the air throbbed.'

It is beyond doubt that the death of Patricia Lynch's father when she was very young and the subsequent nomadic life on which she and her mother embarked are reflected in these images and symbols of emigration. But they also lie behind many of her straightforward 'adventure' stories, where young protagonists (frequently orphans), are portrayed as wanderers in search of domestic comfort and acceptance, forced *en route* to contend with rejection, loneliness and occasionally maltreatment and having as their initial guides only the ambiguities of the signposts and cross-roads with which their landscapes are dotted.

Thus, Brede O'Donnell's story in the 1964 novel *The House by Lough Neagh* sees the heroine's bid to escape from her mean-spirited Cousin Martha in Belfast to her warm-hearted aunt and uncle in rural Co. Antrim and, eventually, to be reunited with her two brothers. And there is a particularly touching treatment of the theme of the isolated orphan in the 1964 novel *Holiday at Rosquin*, where Bernie Nagle attains a measure of self-esteem and dignity through her evolving friendship with Garry Doran, a young boy confined to a wheelchair: the parallel situations of the 'outsider' child are handled with sympathy and conviction, resulting in one of the most accomplished of Lynch's realistic fictions.

In the quarter of a century which has elapsed since Patricia Lynch's death Irish children's literature, in terms of both quantity and quality, has grown to an extent which she could hardly have foreseen. Today's children are accustomed to a different kind of fiction, one which allegedly mirrors faithfully their own time and their own preoccupations. There have, in the shift towards greater social realism, been losses and gains, but the greatest of the former has been in the diminishing recognition of the sheer wildness and rumbustiousness of children's imaginations. In an article entitled 'There Is a Place for Fantasy', published in 1958, Patricia Lynch wrote that, 'Imagination means looking deeper and seeing beyond the veil'. In the best of her work she never forgot the truth of this observation or failed to translate it into practice.

Robert Dunbar
Dublin 1998

EILEEN AND SEAMUS
MEET THE TINKERS

from *The Turf-Cutter's Donkey* (1934)

Eileen and Seamus live with their parents near a bog where their father cuts his turf. They are happy children but they have a secret dream. They would love to have their very own donkey. They could ride it to school and it could also help their father by carrying sods of turf. But how could they afford a donkey? One day on the way to school Eileen finds a little silver teapot that sets her and her brother off on an unexpected adventure ...

Eileen and Seamus lived in a cabin just beyond the cross-roads at the edge of the great bog. The cabin was so low and the thatch so covered with grass and daisies, that a stranger would never have found it only that the walls were whitewashed.

Their father was a turf-cutter, but he knew so many songs to sing and so many tunes to whistle that he hadn't a deal of time for turf-cutting. Then there were the wet days and the cold days, as well as the holidays and the Sundays when it wasn't possible to work. But they had a grand little red cow from Kerry, an elegant pink pig in a neat, tidy sty, when the creature would stay there, and any number of hens and chickens, so they didn't do too badly.

Their mother made lace, beautiful lace – moss roses, shamrocks and butterflies joined by a network of fine chains. When she had finished a piece she sold it on Fair Day at the town on the other side of the flat-topped mountain.

Round the cabin were piles of turf where the children played. The road ran past their home, right across the bog, and that was where they loved to be. In winter it was wild and bleak, but in summer it was white with canavan, the lovely bog-cotton, and the golden flags grew in the pools. There were treacherous green patches and holes so deep there was no bottom to them, but there were paths for those who knew, and trickling streams, and the wind which blew over it was fragrant.

Eileen and Seamus loved watching their father cut the soft brown turf with his slane, the long, sharp, cutting spade, and spread the oblong sods out to dry. First he piled them in threes, each leaning against the others so that the air could get all round them. Then they were gathered in heaps, and when they were quite dry they had to be loaded on carts and taken down to the great stack by the canal. Once a week a barge came and carried the turf away. Sometimes the captain allowed the children to travel with him as far as the lock, and

Seamus made up his mind that when he was a man he would live on a barge and go all over the country instead of staying in a cabin, which never went anywhere.

'If only we had a little donkey!' said Eileen. 'I would love a little grey donkey! He could carry us to school and back, drag our turf home whenever we wanted some, and we could build him a grand little house with sods of turf.'

'And where would the likes of us be getting a donkey?' asked Seamus.

One morning they helped their father load the cart, said goodbye to their mother, to Big Fella the dog, and Rose the cat, and set off down to the canal. Eileen had a sore toe, so she sat on top of the turf while her father pulled and Seamus pushed.

It was a bright, sunshiny day and Eileen was sorry when she saw how hot and red they were.

'If only we had the tiniest little donkey!' she said to herself. 'A little grey donkey!'

And she longed for that donkey more than she had ever longed for anything before.

At last they came to the canal.

The turf-cutter sat down to rest, for there was all the day before him for work, while Eileen and Seamus took the road to school.

But Eileen's sore toe hurt her so much that she limped.

'We'll never get to school at this rate of going!'

exclaimed Seamus. 'Stand on this stone, Eileen, put your arms around my neck and I'll give you a piggy-back!'

Eileen stood up on the stone, but instead of putting her arms around her brother's neck, she pointed along the path.

'Look, Seamus! Look at the dotey little teapot!'

Seamus looked and there, shining and gleaming in every dent of it, was a battered silver teapot, no bigger than a breakfast cup!

He was so surprised he stood there staring, but Eileen jumped down from the stone and picked up the little teapot.

The lid was fastened securely and was tied to both the spout and the handle with a stout piece of string. As Seamus tried to untie the knots a great uproar came from a clump of trees at the bend of the road.

They heard the shouts of men and women, the screams of children, the barking of dogs and, worst of all, the sound of a stick beating someone.

Eileen turned pale. Seamus clasped the teapot tightly.

'It's the tinkers!' whispered Eileen.

'Don't make a sound!' said Seamus softly. 'We'll take the path up the mountain and they'll never set eyes on us.'

He went first and Eileen, forgetting her sore toe, followed as quickly as she could. They were so nervous that they tripped over brambles, crushed dried twigs underfoot and sent stones clattering down the mountain, but none of these sounds could be heard because of the tinkers' clamour.

Suddenly Seamus stopped. Through a gap in the bushes they could see right down into the tinkers' encampment.

A cart with a broken wheel was propped on a log. The tinkers were preparing to leave and the cart was loaded with their saucepans and kettles, while a bony horse stood in the shafts.

Some of the tinkers were searching among the bushes, others stood arguing, while a tall, ragged man, with a bushy black beard and a bright yellow handkerchief twisted about his head, was making a speech. At the end of every sentence he brought down a big stick on the back and sides of a donkey which was fastened to a tree.

The children had never seen such a thin, miserable donkey before. It did not move even when it felt the stick, but stood still, its head hanging down, its long ears folded over each other. Its tail was like a bit of cord, and its mane was all worn away.

'Oh, the poor donkey!' cried Eileen, bursting into tears. 'The poor little donkey!'

At that moment all the tinkers stopped their noise and Eileen's voice could be heard quite distinctly.

Some of the tinkers peered into the trees,

others looked along the path, but the tall man stared straight up at the children.

'Come down along here out of that!' he roared.

The children turned and ran – the other way. As Seamus darted between the bushes, the sun gleamed on the silver teapot he still carried.

'After him!' cried the tall tinker. 'He's stolen our pot!'

Seamus laughed. He and Eileen were the best runners for miles around. The tinkers could never catch them! But as he laughed Eileen knocked her sore toe against a rock and, with a scream of pain, fell on her knees.

Seamus stopped and pulled her up.

'We must hide!' he said.

But what was happening to the tinkers?

The quiet donkey, with a sudden tug, broke the rope which fastened it to the tree. As the tall man who had been beating it ordered the tinkers to follow the children, it gave a plunge, kicked up its heels, sent the tinkers tumbling over one another, and rushed up the hill-side.

As it passed, Seamus caught the broken rope and sprang on its back, while Eileen scrambled up behind.

Raising his hand above his head, Seamus flung the silver teapot towards the tinkers.

'Take the pot!' he shouted. 'We'll keep the donkey!'

THE CABIN IN THE MOUNTAINS

from *King of the Tinkers* (1938)

The Widow Fahy and her son Miheal are poor people who have to work hard to make a living. Their only enemy is the man known as 'Yellow Handkerchief', who has been quarrelling with them for a long time. Yellow Handkerchief is the leader, or 'king', of the tinkers. These were the men and women who travelled around the Irish countryside, sometimes mending pots and pans, and usually looked on with suspicion by the settled people. But, in spite of the mean 'king', Miheal and his mother are happy together in their little cabin.

Miheal was the son of a fiddler. He lived with his mother, the Widow Fahy, in a stone cabin hidden away in the mountains. Even the roof was made of long slabs of stone and the little house was so strong that the worst gale of winter never so much as rattled the windows.

The door was painted green and had two windows on one side, one on the other. A red rose was planted by the door and jasmine grew around each window. There were always clean, white muslin curtains to the windows and Miheal thought that everyone who passed must envy him and his mother their snug home.

But very few passed that way, for the cabin was a long distance from the road and there wasn't another dwelling within sight or sound. For days at a time they would see no-one, except maybe a mountain sheep or one of the rough, shaggy goats that wandered the mountains.

Yet Miheal was never lonely, for at night when they sat by the glowing turf fire, after they had eaten their supper, his mother told him stories. These were always about the mountains and the rebels who had hidden there in the olden times. She told him too that on Hallow E'en and Midsummer Eve the gods and heroes of ancient days came back and were seen marching and riding through the valleys. Then there were the leprechauns who could be heard mending shoes on hot, still days and strangers who had come from foreign parts – she had a story for each one of them. But the stories he liked most of all were about his father, Fahy the Fiddler, who had been the best fiddler of the whole countryside.

When Miheal was lifting the potatoes, or cutting the turf, or just scrambling among the rocks, he thought of the men who had taken refuge in caves and wished he could help them. He listened for the leprechaun and planned all he would do when he won a crock of gold. And when he looked down at the twisting path which led to the road, he imagined himself journeying away to meet all kinds of adventures.

They were very poor, were Miheal and his mother. They had neither a donkey, nor a cow, nor even a pig. To be sure, they had all the turf they could use for the cutting and drying so they were never without a fire, and they had a goat to give them milk – a quiet, gentle creature who was always within call. There was a potato patch on the bit of level ground at the side of the cabin, as well as a row of rhubarb, a bed of winter greens and six gooseberry bushes. For all that they would have been hungry many a time but for the widow's knitting.

She was always making socks and mufflers. When she could buy a big hank of wool she would make a jumper or a pullover; then she bought a piece of bacon and they had grand dinners until the last bit was eaten. She kept her needles and her wool in the pockets of her apron so that she need never lose a moment.

Miheal helped all he could. He held the skeins for his mother to wind the wool into a big, soft ball and at night, when the cabin door was closed against the wind or the mist, he made clothes pegs from the bits of wood he dug out with the turf.

The widow sat on the big creepy and Miheal sat on the small one with the short leg that made it rock every time he moved. He tried to shape the pegs as fast as his mother's needles darted in and out. But when the story she was telling grew exciting, his knife ceased cutting and he forgot everything but the tale he was hearing.

Then he would cut away very quickly until she said:

'Time for bed, Miheal avic.'

He rubbed the pegs he had made on a rough stone to smooth away splinters, gathered up his bits of wood and put them on the window-sill ready for next day.

One day Miheal's mother discovered that she hadn't a scrap of wool left.

'Isn't that very queer,' she said to Miheal. 'I was sure I had enough for a pair of socks as well as a muffler, and what will we do for tea and sugar, not to mind the bag of flour, if I have no wool?'

Miheal helped her search in the press against the wall, the chest under the window, the shelves behind the curtain at the foot of her bed. There wasn't the smallest ball of wool to be found. Suddenly he dropped on his knees and pulled out a cardboard box from under the settle bed where he slept.

'Look, Mother,' he said. 'Couldn't you knit something with all these bits?'

When Miheal was quite a little boy he was always making reins with the ends of wool left over. By the time he was too old for such an amusement he had collected a box of pieces and there they were!

The widow laughed.

'They're too small, Miheal avic. What could I make with them at all?'

But she was running her fingers through the heap, pulling out the longest pieces and winding them as they came, red, blue, black, yellow, white, green, brown.

At last she had the biggest ball of wool Miheal had ever seen and she began to knit.

'Is it a stocking you're knitting?' asked Miheal when his mother had been knitting for hours.

'Who would wear stockings with all the colours of the rainbow?' she asked, laughing.

Then Miheal laughed too, for only a giant could have worn such a huge stocking.

'It's a pullover,' he said, and wished it was for him, though his blue jersey was thick and strong.

The widow worked so quickly that before nightfall the pullover was half made. She went on knitting while Miheal made the tea and boiled the potatoes for their supper and while he made pegs and she told him the story of the leprechaun with only one leg, her fingers were pushing the needles in and out.

When he was in bed Miheal dreamed that when the pullover was finished he put it on and went to the fair in it. He looked so grand that everyone thought him a rich farmer and offered him horses and cows and pigs. He jumped on a black horse but as he rode away the man who owned it ran after Miheal for the money, and when he had none the people at the fair pulled Miheal from the horse and called him a beggar. He woke still hearing their jeers.

To his amazement there was his mother sitting by the fire and, as he looked, she made the last stitch and held up the finished pullover.

It was a wonderful pullover, but Miheal was glad to wear his old blue jersey. He pulled it on quickly.

'If you hurry, Miheal, you'll be in time for Jerry Shaughnessy,' said the widow.

Jerry Shaughnessy was the higgler who went round the countryside collecting eggs and selling them at the fair. He was a great friend of the widow and Miheal. When they had anything to sell, Miheal would go down to the cross-roads and wait for Jerry. He gave the knitting and the pegs as well as a list of the groceries to the higgler, who took their work along to the town and brought them back all they wanted.

The only fault Miheal could find with Jerry was that he would never take him to the town. He often gave Miheal a ride as far as the pine wood, but never once had Miheal been able to coax a ride down the other road from him.

Jerry always came by the cross-roads very early, so Miheal had just time to wash and comb his hair, drink a cup of hot tea and gobble a thick slice of dry soda cake.

'There'll be butter for us in plenty when Jerry sells that pullover,' said the widow proudly, as she wrapped it carefully in a big sheet of brown paper and put it into the market basket.

Miheal had tied his pegs in a bundle and he put them on top of the pullover.

'Mother,' he said, 'isn't it queer how Jerry will never give me a lift into the town?'

'How could he?' she asked. 'Isn't his cart full up with all the eggs he collects? Jerry is very good to us. Don't vex him now.'

Miheal picked up the basket and ran down the path, waving goodbye.

The widow stood at the half-door watching until the boy was hidden in the mist.

It was lucky that Miheal knew the path so well he didn't need to see his way, for the mist was thick and still. He was breathless when at last he jumped out upon the road, but the wet cold made him shiver.

'That's the worst mist I've ever seen,' thought Miheal, and he looked back longingly, wishing he were sitting by the snug hearth, but the cabin had vanished and, though Miheal could point to the exact spot where his home should be, there was nothing but a grey cloud which hid road and mountains.

'When the sun rises the mist will fade,' Miheal told himself, trying to be cheerful. 'It must be terrible early.'

He walked in the middle of the road hoping a drover would come along and be company for him. But Miheal was the only one abroad.

His bare feet made no sound. The birds were silent, and even the great waterfall beyond his home sounded faint and very far away.

'If I had a dog,' thought Miheal, 'he'd be with me and I wouldn't mind the mist a bit.'

Miheal began to plan all the tricks he would teach his dog, when he had one, and he thought of the tune he would play when he had a fiddle like his father. He forgot the mist. He forgot to keep watch out for the cross-roads but went along, swinging the basket.

He didn't know he was near the signpost until he bumped into it, and then he was so busy rubbing his head he forgot the dog and the tricks he meant to teach it.

FOUR WHITE SWANS

from *The Grey Goose of Kilnevin* (1939)

When Jim Daly the farmer decides not to take his little grey goose to Kilnevin Fair she makes up her mind to go there by herself. On the way, she meets a variety of companions, including the Ballad Singer, his son, Fergus, and the apple woman. She also meets a young girl called Sheila. Sheila names the little goose Betsy, and they are soon good friends. Betsy has the power of talking to humans; she speaks as if she were an old woman from West Cork. (The special words and phrases she uses are explained in the glossary at the back of the book.) Following a heavy snowstorm the friends become separated and Sheila is almost captured by her unkind red-haired guardian, Fat Maggie. Betsy comes to her rescue and both of them attempt a daring escape by diving into the rough waters of the lake.

'Do you know where we're going?' asked Sheila. Betsy was tingling with delight as she bobbed along.

'Sorra one o' me knows or cares,' she hissed.

'I'm not cold and I'm not so very tired,' said Sheila, 'but I'm starving. And, Betsy, I've money in me pocket that I never had a chance to spend. Isn't that terrible?'

'Isn't it a pity ye can't feed like a goose?' asked Betsy. 'Ye wouldn't believe the wonderful fine atin there does be in the soft juicy mud. But what can we do now? Keep a watch out, an if ye set eyes on a cabin, or a village, or any kind of place where human crathures live, we'll go ashore an ye can get what ye want.'

'I wonder if Fergus and the Ballad Singer and the apple woman are looking for me,' sighed Sheila. 'I do wish they could find us.'

The little girl and the grey goose floated in silence. The moon was high and full and the wet trees and earth glistened as if they had been painted with silver.

'If I had just a mouthful to eat and I knew me friends would find me, I'd love this,' said Sheila. 'But I'm sorry the snow has gone.'

'Ye can't swim in snow,' argued Betsy.

'Did you hear that?' asked Sheila.

'I hear the water rushin along an suckin into the earth an dripping from the trees an the rocks,' replied Betsy. 'Was it ere a one of them noises?'

Sheila shook her head.

'No, but the sound of a song.'

Even Betsy could hear voices singing.

'Mebbe tis that old Ballad Singer,' she hissed. 'Ye'd think that fella was a singin bird the way he does be always givin out a tune.'

'It isn't the Ballad Singer. I wish it was,' said Sheila sadly.

Uprooted trees floated by. Great sods of earth held together with grass and creeping plants crashed into the water. Little foam-crested waves danced along, but Sheila wasn't minding them. She was straining her eyes to see into the deep shadows and she listened to the song which came down the wind with words and bits of the tune tossed away.

'Can you hear what they're singing, Betsy?' whispered Sheila.

The grey goose splashed her bill in the water.

'I'm not over good at understandin the talk of human crathures, barrin yerself, Sheila,' she mumbled. 'But sure we're ridin along to whoever it is as fast as the stream can carry us. Ye'll hear all ye want in next to no time.'

'Something about four white swans,' murmured Sheila.

Betsy stood up on her tail and flapped her wings.

'Four white swans!' she hissed. 'Watch out, Sheila, watch out! For if we miss this chance we'll be terrible sad and sorry.'

Sheila shook the water from her eyes.

'What are you talking about, Betsy?' she demanded.

On rushed the stream, and at the foot of a high rock, overhanging the flood, Sheila saw something white crouched under a tree.

'Is them the four swans?' asked Betsy, swimming towards the shore.

Sheila shook her head.

'I can't see; yes, I can! They're not swans, Betsy, but four children, and they're waving to us.'

Betsy hissed loudly in disappointment.

'I was hoping I'd meet them, after the way the wild geese were tellin me of the wonders they are. Still, there's time yet.'

Sheila found it hard work to reach the bank. The current was strong and she was being swept past the rock when the four children leaped down and pulled her out of the water.

The grey goose needed no help. She bobbed off the water on to the land, wriggled, and hissed, standing on one leg.

Sheila lay on the ground, gasping for breath and shaking her hair.

'Oo! It's cold!' she cried.

She looked up at the children. The tallest was a girl, the other three were boys. They were so thin and white that in the moonlight it wasn't easy to see them. They wore short, white tunics which were pasted against their bodies by the wind and rain, and their long, golden hair was as wet as Sheila's.

'Are you lost, too?' she asked.

She was delighted with them, for their eyes were friendly and smiling.

'We aren't lost,' replied the girl slowly. 'But we cannot get back.'

'Is there someone chasing you?' asked Sheila, sitting up. 'Is it the red-haired woman? She's chasing us, and she's terrible.'

'Long ago there was a woman with red-gold hair who harmed us,' said the girl. 'But we are no longer afraid of her. All we fear is losing our feather cloaks. Without them we are so helpless. We cannot even swim to them.'

Sheila looked at the children in wonder. Though they were shivering and seemed like shadows in the wild night she had never seen anyone so lovely before.

'Where is your home?' asked Sheila.

'Where the silver path meets the gold, and light and darkness are one,' replied the four, speaking all together.

'I heard tell o' that place,' hissed Betsy, hopping up and down with excitement. 'Now, it wasn't the old gander told me. That was a powerful clever old gander where I used to be an I wid him in a big red house. But I don't believe he ever heard tell of it. No! Twas the wild geese, an they told me twas the home of the –'

The girl bent down.

'Didn't the wild geese tell you not to reveal your knowledge?' she asked.

Betsy hung down her head.

'Bedad they did!' she answered.

Sheila looked at the girl. Then she looked at Betsy.

'Why shouldn't I know?' she thought.

'Where I come from,' said Sheila, 'there was a dote of a harbour and the mountains go down to the sea. There was a coloured window with four white swans. It was a lovely window, but I wasn't happy living in that house. The woman wasn't kind to me.'

Sheila thought how long ago it was since she had left the House of the Four Swans and she wondered would she ever go back.

'Where are your feather cloaks?' she asked the children.

The girl pointed out across the tossing water, down the gleaming track made by the moonlight. But as far as Sheila could see there were waves, leaping and foaming.

'I can swim,' she said. 'I've never been far from the shore and only when the sea was quiet. But I can swim.'

'There aren't many swimmers can best me,' boasted Betsy. 'But that's a quare, wild sea.'

'Weren't they foolish to leave their cloaks behind them?' thought Sheila. 'And how did they come here?'

But she did not like to question the strangers.

'I'd be glad to help you,' she said. 'But I'd be afraid to swim out there in the moonlight, and the water is so rough and I'm cold and hungry and sleepy.'

Yet there she was, slipping back into the water.

'You might be needing the basket,' the girl told Sheila, and pushed it after her.

The basket led the way. Sheila tried to reach it.

'Never mind the basket,' advised Betsy, who kept close to Sheila. 'Let yerself lie on the water and just give a bit of a push now an then.'

They climbed the waves and sank into the hollows as if they were flying.

'How will we get back?' Sheila asked Betsy. 'The tide will be against us.'

'Sure a tide is always turnin,' chuckled the grey goose. She was delighted to be swimming with Sheila in the moonlight.

Then Sheila forgot to worry. Low down in the sky great clouds were massed. They were formed into great mountains with deep valleys opening between and, perched on a high, jutting crag, Sheila saw a glittering castle. As the white-topped waves crashed on the shore the wind swept off the foam, tumbling it along the strand until each fragment galloped away as a white horse.

The sun was rising and a path of gold blotted out the track of moonlight.

Sheila looked back, but she saw only the tossing waves.

The grey goose kept close to Sheila and there wasn't a single hiss from her.

They came nearer to a bank of sand reaching out into the water.

'Can ye see what I see?' the grey goose hissed very softly, as if she were afraid of being overheard.

'I see a heap of white feathers lying on the shore,' whispered Sheila. 'Can ye guess what the wild geese told me?' hissed Betsy.

Sheila nodded.

'I know now. We've come to the home of the Swan Children.'

A wave tumbled them gently out on the warm sand, basket and all.

Sheila rolled over and over. 'Isn't it grand to have the sun shining again!' she cried. 'And there's a path. It leads to the green castle with the coppery roofs.'

'When I encounter them wild geese again I'll have a terrible long story to tell,' chuckled Betsy. 'But I wish I knew the whole of it. Ye know a mint of stories, Sheila. Do ye know one about them childer?'

'I think I do,' said Sheila. 'But swim closer, Betsy, I don't want to talk out loud.'

Betsy swam as close to Sheila as she could, for the feather cloak spread out over the surface of the water and the little girl sat up as though she were in a boat.

'They are the Swan Children, I'm sure of that,' she said, leaning back and snuggling her head against the soft feathers, while the basket floated on one side of her and the grey goose on the other.

'Sure, they're the Swan Children,' agreed Betsy, 'but there's more to it than that.'

'Once upon a time,' began Sheila, and the grey goose waggled her tail and hissed with pleasure, for she knew that this was the proper way to tell a story, 'there was a king in ancient Ireland and his name was Lir.'

'I never heard tell o' that one before,' hissed Betsy happily.

'Lir had four children,' said Sheila, 'there was a girl, now what was her name? It's a hard one to remember, but I know I heard it once. Fi-on-uala – that was the name – and her three brothers. Their mother was dead but they had a stepmother who was jealous of them.'

'The quare crathure!' hissed Betsy. 'Is it a true story ye're tellin me?'

'Of course it is!' exclaimed Sheila indignantly. 'Aren't the children over there waiting for us?

Didn't you see them with your own two eyes?'

'I did indeed, but how would I know their story? The wild geese never told me that!' hissed Betsy. 'But they spoke very well of them.'

'One day,' continued Sheila, 'their stepmother took the children out for a drive in her chariot. They went on for miles and miles until they came to a lake among the mountains with a beach like the one we've just come from. Fionuala and the boys wanted to go swimming, and while they were running down to the water the stepmother told the man who drove the chariot that he must kill them.'

''Pon me word!' cried Betsy in horror, 'that one was no better than that red-headed villyan of a wumman that does be chasin us!'

Sheila nodded.

'She was wicked, but she was beautiful. She had hair that shone red like the sun and it was so long it fell round her like a cloak. Her eyes were deep green like the ocean, and her teeth –'

'Go on wid the story, Sheila allanna,' begged the little grey goose. 'We'll be back wid them childer before I know their sad history. Never mind the looks of the crathure!'

'The driver was a kind man, and he was fond of the poor children,' said Sheila. 'He wouldn't kill them and he told the stepmother she was a wicked, unkind woman. He called Fionuala to swim away and take her brothers with her. They came swimming back, because they couldn't understand what he was saying. Before they could reach the shore the cruel queen waved her hands and sang a spell which changed the children into swans.'

'Wasn't it well for them?' hissed Betsy. 'I wouldn't be complainin if I found meself turned into a swan this blessed minit, so I wouldn't.'

'Swans should be swans and children should be children,' declared Sheila. 'Mebbe you wouldn't mind being turned into a swan, but how would you like to be turned into a little girl?'

'Sorra wan o' me knows,' hissed the grey goose. 'Mebbe I wouldn't notice the change.'

'I'll hurry up and tell you the end,' said Sheila quickly. 'The children were swans for hundreds and hundreds of years until the coming of St Patrick. He lifted the spell, so that sometimes they are really children, but to make up for all they suffered they can be swans when they like.'

'Isn't it wonderful to know all that,' hissed Betsy. 'Where did ye larn it, Sheila?'

'I read it in a book,' explained Sheila. 'But I never dreamed I'd know them and wear a feather cloak so that I can ride on the water like a swan.'

'Bring our cloaks before the moonlight goes,' called a voice over the water. 'Quickly! Quickly!'

Sheila hadn't noticed that they had left the sunshine and the warmth behind and now they were back where the snow was melting and the cold rain dripped from the trees and swelled the flood.

The moon was fading. The silver path which had guided them could scarcely be seen and Sheila knew the day on this side would soon be dawning.

'Quick! Quick!' came the voice once more. 'Bring our cloaks before the sun rises, or we are lost indeed.'

'Tis the Swan Childer callin,' warned Betsy. 'Hurry, Sheila! Tis only ye can help them now.'

The feathered cloak covered Sheila from head to foot. She was floating quickly towards the bank, but it was still out of sight.

'I must go faster,' she exclaimed. 'But how can I swim in this!'

Yet when she pressed back the water with her hands, she shot forward so that Betsy was left behind. But, fast as Sheila went, the basket kept up with her.

'I'm coming!' she called. 'I'm coming!'

She could see the four children now. They were wading into the water and, to prevent themselves from being carried away, they clung together.

They're like shadows, thought Sheila, fearing they would vanish before she reached them.

She was proud as she swept up to the bank. She pulled off the cloak and flung it to the girl, then tugged the other cloaks from the basket and gave them to the boys.

As they wrapped themselves in the cloaks, a golden ray streamed across the sky and the sun climbed up over the water.

'Bedad, ye were just in time, Sheila,' gasped Betsy, bobbing along breathlessly. 'But tis a desprit pity ye couldn't keep the cloak. Ye'd make as good a swan as any one of them, so ye would.'

Sheila stared in wonder for, instead of four shivering children, four stately white swans floated on the water.

'I knew you were the Swan Children!' declared Sheila. 'Now, tell me, when I wore the cloak did I look like a swan?'

'Indade an ye didn't look like a swan,' hissed Betsy. 'Ye looked just like me own Sheila wrapped in a feather cloak.'

'We must return now,' said the biggest swan. 'But for you, Sheila, we might have had to wander on the earth as children for many years.'

'Don't you want to be children?' asked Sheila.

The swans looked at one another. The three smaller ones were drifting away, but the big swan swam backwards and forwards.

'There are times when we long to come back,' explained the big swan. 'But our coming brings storm and snow. If you had been afraid and we had been forced to stay without our cloaks, great sorrow and suffering would have come upon the land.'

The three small swans were far away now and

the swan Fionuala turned to follow them.

'Is there anything you have a great wish for, Sheila?' she asked. 'You were kind to us.'

Sheila grew red.

'I'd love to be beautiful like you were,' she said quickly, 'to have blue eyes and long golden curls.'

'Are you sure you want that?' asked the swan, as a white mist came crowding over the water so that they could scarcely see one another.

'Think again, Sheila,' begged Betsy. 'Don't be axin for rubbish. Tis a chance to get what ye really want.'

Sheila was ashamed.

'Of course I want most of all to find me friends,' said Sheila. 'But the fox promised he'd show me the way they went. Then I must find Bridgie Swallow, or dear knows what Maggie Fagan will do to me when she gets me back, and I do want to go back.'

The mist was so thick that the three swans were quite hidden and Fionuala became a dim shape while Sheila was speaking.

'You'll need help to get back – but first you must cross over,' came the swan girl's voice, so faintly that Sheila wasn't sure that she heard properly.

'Cross over? We have crossed over. Didn't we swim there and back?' she murmured, feeling puzzled.

The mist was thick around her. Sheila took one step and her feet were in the water.

'Keep still!' hissed the grey goose.

Sheila was frightened, for the mist was like a blanket pressing close and wet against her eyes.

'Where are you, Betsy?' she whispered.

'In the basket, allanna, right here forninst ye. Stoop down an reach out,' hissed Betsy.

Sheila stooped down and reached out.

'No! No! Ye're all the wrong way,' chuckled the grey goose. 'Right round this way.'

Sheila swung round.

'No! No! No! Tis the other way I am. Ah, that's better! A bit lower down. Mind me eye, Sheila!'

SHADOWS ON THE COURTYARD

from *Fiddler's Quest* (1941)

In the 1930s and 1940s many people left Ireland for America. They believed that they would make their fortunes there and return home rich. Ethne Cadogan and her father are poor so he travels to America hoping to become a wealthy man. He tells her that she must stay in Dublin, in the home of the Rafferty family, until she hears from the mysterious 'King' Cadogan of Inishcoppal, her grandfather, whom she has never met. But Dublin is a dangerous place. It is known as 'the City of Troubles' because of the fighting between the Irish rebels and the British soldiers. Ethne does not understand 'the Troubles', but she is about to have a close encounter with them.

A moonbeam falling across her face woke Ethne. She lay with half-opened eyes, looking into the darkened room. Presently she saw another bed against the inner wall and two heads side by side on the pillow. A voice whispered:

'Are you awake, Nono?'

'I am not!' was the answer. 'Go to sleep, Eily!'

'Tell me a story, Nono, please!'

'I will not. Be quiet, or you'll wake Ethne!'

There was silence for a while and now Ethne could see that she was lying on a narrow bed close up to a window looking on the courtyard. She remembered coming in with Nono when the last of the neighbours had gone and leaving Mrs Rafferty by the fire, drinking the last cup of tea.

She looked anxiously around for her violin and smiled contentedly when she saw it on a wooden chest beside her open suitcase and her neatly folded clothes. Her best frock, the black velvet one with a lace collar, hung from a hook on the wall at the foot of the bed. Beside it was the old gold silk frock her father had brought her from Paris. It was short for her now, but it was the loveliest frock she had ever possessed and she was sure she would never part with it. On the other side her green dressing-gown swung slightly in the chill wind blowing in at the open window. That came from Buda-Pesth and the slippers to match were still unpacked.

'Unsettled creatures like ourselves must travel light,' Miles Cadogan had told his daughter. And she was proud that all her possessions, or nearly all, would go into a suitcase.

She regretted the thick, blue school coat and the rug which her father had refused to let her bring away from St Joseph's.

'The coat's an atrocity!' he declared. 'Ye might as well tie a label to her arm with "schoolgirl" written on it, and who wants a rug?'

'Why shouldn't I look like a schoolgirl?' Ethne wanted to know. 'I am one.'

Miles didn't bother to answer that.

She thought over the great times she and her father had had together. How often he had told her how they'd 'go back' one day and stay at the Shelbourne and drive through the Phoenix Park on a side-car and listen to the wonderful singing at the Pro-Cathedral. And now she was in Dublin alone!

Ethne was surprised that she didn't feel unhappy, or even lonesome. She was making friends. She was finding her own way about the world. When she met her father again she would have adventures of her own to tell him, not just the stories of school life which he never pretended to find interesting.

Without lifting her head she could see out of the window. There were no lights in the houses, but the yard was bright and the cobbles were silver blobs. The big cat, Laery, leaped from one of the low roofs and, running round and round, chased his tail. Suddenly he stiffened and, head bent sideways, listened. Then, as suddenly, he stood on his hind legs and danced with his shadow. It lay black on the silvered cobbles and Ethne hummed a tune in her head that went with the dance.

Another shadow lay black on the cobbles. The cat sprang back to the roof and crouched there, watching. A man, tall, thin, his hat pulled over his eyes, his coat collar turned up, stood in the gateway. Very softly he whistled a few bars of a tune and Ethne recognised the song the ballad singer on the quay had been singing when she was outside Andy Dolan's corner shop.

He leaned waiting against the wall reading in a book he had taken from his pocket. A door nearby opened and closed. Ethne saw Eamon Rafferty crossing the courtyard. The stranger came to meet him and they walked back talking, their heads close together until they came to a halt beside Ethne's window.

They were so close that, but for the glass, she could have touched them. A murmur came from them, so faint that Eily and Nono could not hear it.

'I do wonder who pushed Eamon in the water,' whispered Eily.

'Tis none of your business. You should be asleep,' Nono told her.

'Mammy doesn't know tis with Nial Desmond Eamon does be, and not with the boat boys at all,' said Eily.

Ethne could see Nono start, but she did not speak.

'Did you tell Ethne you dreamed of her coming?' asked Eily.

'I did not!' replied Nono. 'And I didn't dream of

her coming. I dreamed a red-headed lady, with a harp under her arm, came into the yard and played to us. Ethne isn't red-headed, she isn't a lady and she doesn't play a harp. And if you say another word I'll be real vexed with you.'

'Wish I had dreams that came true,' sighed Eily.

'You heard what I said,' Nono reminded her.

They lay silent. Ethne raised herself on her elbow and peeped between the curtains at the speakers outside. To her surprise, while she had been listening to the sisters, the ballad singer in the black shawl had come into the courtyard.

Bare feet tiptoed across the room and, leaning over Ethne's bed, Nono looked out at her brother and his companions. As she moved away, her troubled eyes saw that Ethne was awake and watching too. She frowned, tiptoed back, bent down over her sister and returned. Eily was asleep at last.

'Did you see Nial Desmond?' she asked Ethne, speaking so softly that only the sharpest ears could hear.

'Is it the man with his hat over his eyes?' whispered Ethne.

Nono nodded and shivered.

'Come in beside me,' suggested Ethne. 'You can see out and keep warm as well.'

They snuggled under the bed-clothes together, while the murmuring outside continued. Once more a door opened and closed. The ballad singer crossed the courtyard and a few moments after the young man walked noiselessly away.

'That was Nial Desmond,' said Nono. 'One day everyone will hear of him.'

'Who is he?' asked Ethne.

They still spoke in whispers, because of Eily and because of the hour. All the night noises of the river came to them clearly and sometimes Ethne thought she could hear the crash of waves.

Nono looked sideways at Ethne. Her face was very serious.

'I can trust you,' she said. 'He is one of the leaders.'

Ethne lay back to listen in comfort. Nono sat up, hugging her knees.

'You know about the rebels, don't you?' she asked. 'There are some on every quay, in every yard. They want to make Ireland free and grand, like in the ancient times. So they have to fight.'

'Do you like fighting?' asked Ethne doubtfully.

'Sometimes you must fight!' declared Nono. 'If you love your country you want her to be free and the only way to get freedom is by fighting. That's what Eamon says. Twas Nial told him and he knows. You do love your country, don't you, Ethne?'

'Indeed I do!' replied Ethne. 'I've always wanted to come back, always!'

Nono nodded.

'I'm glad you're back,' she said, kindly. 'Well, you can't fight without arms, so Nial and two or mebbe three others captured a whole pile of rifles and revolvers and guns and ammunition!'

'What's ammunition?' Ethne wanted to know.

Nono was appalled at such ignorance.

'You really don't know what ammunition is?' she demanded.

'Not exactly. How would I?' Ethne pointed out. 'I've never been before where there was fighting and in school they don't tell you about the things that matter. You tell me.'

'Ammunition is bullets and cartridges to put in the rifles and revolvers, of course,' explained Nono. 'Well, someone told on Nial and the soldiers, or mebbe they were only policemen, came to arrest him. He saw them coming and climbed out through a back window. But they heard him and dashed round the house. He went over a wall and they fired. One bullet slit the shoulder of his coat but he got away and he's been on the run ever since.'

'If they caught him, what would they do to him?' Ethne wanted to know.

'Shut him up in prison, or mebbe shoot him!' whispered Nono.

Her voice shook and Ethne squeezed her hand to show sympathy. It must be terrible to be in a prison cell with iron bars to the windows. She had passed by a prison once and the big gloomy building had terrified her.

'He's always on the watch,' said Nono breathlessly. 'He never knows when he'll be stopped on the street or they'll find out where he lives – and Eamon watches for him.'

'Is he Nial's friend?' asked Ethne.

'He's a rebel too,' Nono told her proudly. 'But he's only a boy. So am I a rebel and so will you be too, Ethne, when you know all about it. Eamon carries messages and Nial Desmond trusts him. Sometimes I help. Mammy doesn't know. She'd be afraid, for us, I mean. But Nial will never let harm come to us. He takes all the risks. There's nothing in the wide world he's afraid of.'

She sank back breathless.

'A man on *The Granuaile* told me that Dublin is the City of the Troubles,' whispered Ethne. 'That means fighting, doesn't it?'

'There's always fighting somewhere,' said Nono wisely. 'I hate it, but I'd do anything for Nial; so would Eamon – he's a hero!'

There came a tap on the door of the room and Nono jumped from the bed.

'It's Eamon and he wants me,' she murmured, her voice thrilling with pride.

She picked up her coat from a chair, pulled it on and, smiling over her shoulder at Ethne, ran out to the other room.

Ethne determined to stay awake until Nono returned. She wanted to hear more about the ballad singer and Eamon and Nial Desmond, but she was too sleepy. Besides there was all tomorrow, and the days until her grandfather's letter came, for questions.

SKY FARM

from *Long Ears: The Story of*
a Little Grey Donkey (1943)

Long Ears has just arrived in the world and
there is much to see and to learn. His
mother, Kattie Duv, is eager to show him
the farm and to introduce him to all the
other animals. Long Ears has to meet the
humans of Sky Farm too – even if they
cannot seem to understand a word he
says! We have met Long Ears before, in the
opening chapter of The Turf-Cutter's
Donkey, when he escaped from the tinkers
with the help of Eileen and Seamus. In this
story, he is only a young foal and does not
yet know what 'tinkers' are.

Once inside the green gate it was as snug a
farm as you could wish to see. There was the
house itself – low and built of great blocks of stone,
whitewashed so often that the cracks were filled in
and the walls smooth as ice.

Ropes were flung over the roof and tied to
pieces of rock to keep the thatch safe in storms,
and the windows were set half-way through the
thick walls.

The sheds, the fowl house and even the pig-sty
were built of stone. Only the dog kennel, painted

green, was of wood, for it was a barrel, wedged with stones to prevent it from rolling.

The farm was right on the mountain-top. There was nothing higher but the clouds, so they called it Sky Farm. Beyond the green gate and below the high rock two paths led downwards, one to the strand, the other to the main road, which went by town and village to the city of Galway.

A wall rose all round and at the side farthest from the green gate was a new shed. It was so new it wasn't even finished, and the door leaned against the opening.

Inside, Kattie Duv, the big, dark donkey, was talking to her young son, who lay on a heap of straw blinking in wonder and trying to listen to all his mother was telling him.

There were so many strange sounds coming from the farmyard that the little donkey was bewildered. He flapped his long ears and cuddled into the straw.

'Come along now an say "Gran mornin" to the neighbours,' said Kattie Duv.

The shed was dark and the little fellow was snug and warm, but Kattie nudged him gently till he stumbled to his feet.

'Tis time ye had a look at the world,' said the big donkey.

Peering out, the young donkey could see right across the yard to the house.

The sun was rising over a distant mountain covered with grey mist, and the yellow roof glittered. The windows were open, and white muslin curtains fluttered against the red ribbons which held them in place.

The little donkey was afraid and drew back.

'Tis a stony farm, sure enough,' said Kattie Duv. 'An a dale too cocked up in the sky for me likin. But the master an the mistress an the old one is kind, dacent people an tis that counts. Never a harsh word from dawn till dark. An the young one, Eileen Óg, isn't too bad at all. Come along, now!'

She thrust against the door, but it was held by a rock and Kattie could not make it budge.

Lifting her head, the big donkey opened her mouth, showing every tooth, and hee-hawed until the little donkey expected the shed to fall in on them.

They heard the sound of running feet, and Kattie gave a last gentle hee-haw.

'Tis the fat, wee one,' she explained. 'She hasn't much sinse, the crathure, but she manes well.'

'I can't open it!' said a voice. 'What shall I do?'

'Wouldn't ye think she'd have enough sinse to go fetch her daddy, or her mammy, or the old mistress!' grumbled Kattie Duv.

'Couldn't you tell her?' asked the little donkey timidly.

'Tell Eileen Óg, is it?' demanded his mother.

'Sure, she doesn't understand our class of talk. Didn't I tell ye the child has no sinse!'

'I'll get me granny!' said Eileen Óg, outside the shed.

The little donkey saw her trotting across the yard, her blue frock blown back, her fair hair streaming on the wind, her bare feet stumbling over the stones, and her two fists clenched with determination.

'I like Eileen Óg,' he told his mother.

Kattie Duv wasn't listening. She was impatient to be out in the yard. There was Eileen Óg coming back and, with her, the old mistress in her neat black dress and her polished shoes, stepping carefully. Yet she reached the shed as quickly as the little girl, who stopped to watch a sunbeam in a puddle, looked into the sty, and listened at the door of the fowl house.

'That one's always the last,' complained Kattie. 'I never knew her like for not keepin her mind on what she should be doin!'

The old mistress pushed away the rock and pulled back the door. Sunlight streamed into the far corners, and a quick wind sent wisps of straw scurrying across the floor.

'Ye're a gran lassie!' said the old woman to Kattie. 'But that's a quare little son ye have. Will ye just take a look at the long ears of him!'

The little donkey was so small and young his

long legs trembled under him as he followed Kattie.

'I love him!' declared Eileen Óg. 'He's a dote!'

And she put her arms round him.

'Aisy, child! Aisy!' cried the old mistress. 'Ye'll terrify the crathure.'

'Long Ears isn't afraid of me!' declared Eileen Óg, and she rubbed her face against his velvety nose.

'Pon me word, ye've named him right!' chuckled her grandmother. 'There's yer name, little fellow – Long Ears!'

Kattie Duv tossed her head with pride as she walked across the yard, the little donkey keeping very close to her. And, where they went, Eileen Óg went too.

The old woman opened the door of the house to let out the ducks and hens and the big brown cock, who had been crowing indignantly for nearly an hour.

He fluttered up on a great stone, flapped his wings and gazed scornfully about the farmyard. The hens cackled with excitement and scratched the soft earth beside the wall.

'Tis takin me young son to see the neighbours I am,' explained Kattie Duv. 'But he's that shy! Say "Gran mornin" to the neighbours now.'

Long Ears hung his head and wouldn't say a word.

'Tis a pity he isn't a cock like me,' said the brown cock, looking down from his perch. 'He's a terrible queer crathure with them long ears!'

Flinging back his head, he crowed proudly: 'Cock-a-doodle-d-o-o.'

'That's a sign he comes from high-class donkeys,' explained Kattie. 'Takes after his father, he does. I've the Spanish strain meself. That's why I'm so dark an quick on me hoofs.'

'Wish I knew what they're saying,' whispered Eileen Óg to Long Ears.

The little donkey gave a tiny hee-haw.

'I've the loudest crow in the world! I'm the finest cock in the world!' boasted the brown cock.

'Don't mind his old chat,' Kattie Duv told her son as she went across the yard to the sty.

The sty had a stone wall round it and plenty of clean straw, but the sow and her thirteen bonaveens liked the end where rain had formed a muddy puddle.

Eileen Óg scrambled onto the stone wall.

'Long Ears has come to see you, Lady!' she told the sow.

'Tis me young son,' explained Kattie Duv. 'Wouldn't it be as well for our childer to be friends seein they'll be livin here beside one another?'

Lady grunted, her bonaveens squealed. Kattie Duv tossed her head indignantly and marched away.

'I never could abide bad manners!' she declared. 'Still, amn't I very foolish to expect anything from a pig barrin a grunt! Sure they know no better!'

Eileen Óg jumped down from the wall.

'Come and talk to the ducks,' she said.

Kattie Duv looked sideways at the little grey donkey.

'D'ye hear that young one tellin me what to do?' she muttered.

But she followed the little girl to the duck pond at the end of the low stone wall. The drake stood on a flat stone where the stream flowed through a hollow and blinked at Eileen Óg and the two donkeys.

'How's yerself?' asked Kattie Duv politely. 'I want everyone to know me fine handsome son. But he's that shy! Still an all he'll grow out of it.'

The drake stood still, smoothing his tail feathers with his orange bill, but the ducks splashed out of the water, quacking and crowding together, standing on one another's feet and looking sideways at the little grey donkey.

'Look at his ears – quack! Look at his ears – quack! quack!' said the ducks.

Long Ears ventured a peep at the quacking ducks.

'I don't like their talk,' he thought. 'There's no sense to it.'

'Tis a gran day we're goin to have, thanks be,' said Kattie Duv to the ducks. 'We'll be movin on.'

The ducks blinked and never stopped quacking, while Eileen Óg, Kattie Duv and the little grey donkey went on.

The cock glared after them from the top of the fowl house.

'Why isn't your son a cock, Kattie Duv?' he demanded. 'I'd teach him to crow. Hasn't he terrible long ears? Cock-a-doodle-d-o-o!'

Kattie Duv stamped crossly but she wanted to keep good friends with her neighbours.

'Don't I agree wid every word ye're after sayin?' she said. 'But we can't all be cocks, nor hins nayther for the matter of that. An, if we could, who'd want to? That's what I'm axin! As for his ears, why wouldn't a donkey have long ears? Isn't it only natural?'

The cock crowed; the hens scratched; the ducks splashed back into the pond. Kattie Duv and Eileen Óg went on to the house, and the little grey donkey kept so close to them that first he bumped into his mother and then into the little girl.

They reached the green barrel and Red Lad, the watch-dog who lived in it, yawned, stretched and stepped out.

'Now he's seen the neighbours, he'd as well know his friends,' said Red Lad, whining gently.

The little donkey liked the dog's friendly eyes.

'Isn't he a fine lump of a lad!' declared the dog, wagging his tail. 'Ye'll be proud of him yet, I'm tellin ye!'

'I like this one,' thought Long Ears. 'He doesn't quack, or crow, or grunt, but he talks sense.'

Kattie Duv tossed her head.

'He's a fine child, if I do say it,' she said proudly. 'He'll be a good runner an a fine jumper, like meself – that's the Spanish strain, ye know.'

Red Lad wagged his tail and laughed, showing all his teeth.

'Isn't that grand! I don't know much about me own family, but if erra one of them did come along, there's a few bones I've buried behind the turf pile and I'd let them help themselves.'

Eileen Óg sat on the barrel, Kattie thrust her head over the half-door, Red Lad stood up on his hind legs beside her and the little grey donkey squeezed in between.

The grandmother was at the fire stirring the pot of porridge which hung on a chain.

'Will ye look what's at the dure!' she cried.

The young mistress, her sleeves rolled up, was making a potato cake at the table by the window.

'If he's not the cute little fella!' she said, laughing. 'By the time Eileen's big enough to go to school he'll be big enough to carry her there.'

The old woman stopped stirring the porridge and pointed with the spoon.

'D'ye see the ears on him! He carries his name on his head – Long Ears!'

'Here's dadda!' called Eileen Óg.

Tim O'Farrell came in at the gateway, his slane over his shoulder, for he had been cutting turf lower down on the mountain.

'What's the crowd?' he asked. Then he saw Long Ears.

'Pon me word, that's a great little lad! He's yours, Eileen. Take good care of him.'

He went into breakfast with the little girl. The two donkeys went back to the shed to their breakfast.

Kattie Duv was terribly proud. She couldn't help wishing her son's ears weren't quite so long, but the people at the house and Red Lad had a great opinion of him and already he had a name.

'An he so young,' she thought.

Long Ears lay on the straw and stretched his legs.

'I like the world,' he thought. 'I wonder if there's much more of it. I like Eileen Óg and I like Red Lad.'

Then he fell asleep.

THE SHADOW PEDLAR

from *The Seventh Pig and
Other Irish Fairy Tales* (1950)

*This is a story about the Sandman's less
well known brother, the Shadow Pedlar.
The Sandman pours dream-sand on
people's eyes to lull them into sleep and
sweet dreams. The job of the Shadow
Pedlar is to go around the country buying
all the dreams that the Sandman needs,
which is not an easy job because dreams
are in great demand. But people like Kevin
Hanlon, who are always day-dreaming,
have a good store of dreams for sale and
the Shadow Pedlar knows what price they
are willing to sell them for.*

Kevin Hanlon was bringing in turf from the big
pile at the side of the cabin.

'Mind now and take dry sods,' his mother called
after him.

He heard her, though the moment he came
through the doorway spray from the rocks below
tossed up in his face, rain dripped noisily from the
overhanging thatch and, as he ran past the
window, the wind tried to draw away the sack he
had thrown over his head and shoulders.

'How can it be Christmas and it raining!' he

grumbled. 'There should be snow at Christmas!'

He grabbed sods from the end of the pile nearest the cabin and quickly packed them in the creel. They were quite dry, and even the brown mould underfoot was sheltered from the rain.

As Kevin went back he bent over the heavy creel. The wind came up behind and pushed him on. But, coming or going, Kevin always looked seaward. Far beyond the grey curtain of rain and spray was Spain, where the sun always shone and grapes and oranges grew like blackberries on brambles.

While rain seeped through the sack and trickled inside his collar Kevin stood there, forgetting that the fire needed turf, forgetting even the weight of the creel. He gazed so hard out to sea he imagined the mist was swept away, the sky became blue and the sun shone.

'Kevin!' called his mother. 'Hurry, lad!'

He started, blinked away the raindrops, and stumbled into the warm room. His father, lounging on the settle, shook his head at him.

'If you must dream,' he said, 'don't do it standing out in the rain.'

'I was just thinking,' explained Kevin.

His brother and sister grinned. John was finishing a set of shelves he was making for his mother's books, and Bridie was putting the last stitches into a pink frock for the baby who lay sucking her thumb and staring up at the old grannie's knitting-needles as they went clack-clack!

Kevin knelt by the hearth to pile the sods against the wall. Even there he could hear the crash of waves upon the shore and the ceaseless scurry of the rain.

'I hate rain!' he told his mother. 'If we can't have sunshine we should have snow. Mammy! Mightn't the rain turn to snow?'

He sat back on his heels and watched the steam pouring from the spout of the big, black kettle hanging over the fire, and sniffed the savoury smell from the salt fish simmering in the pan on the hearth.

His mother laughed at his serious face and tousled hair with bits of turf sticking in it. Kevin never minded his mother's laughter. He laughed too.

'The wind is blowing the rain away,' she said. 'Twill be drying up before we've eaten our tea. I can't promise you snow for tomorrow but there'll be frost tonight and a full moon. Isn't that grand now for Christmas Eve?'

Mr Hanlon reached up to the high mantelpiece for his pipe.

'Let's hope we'll have a good Fair,' he muttered, as Bridie picked up a piece of red turf with the heavy iron tongs and held it while he puffed and puffed. 'I've a grand load of onions and we'll need all we can get for them.'

'There's a basket of thyme and sage all tied in bundles,' Mrs Hanlon told him. 'Grannie fixed them herself. You can always sell onions and herbs at the Christmas Fair!'

'Then we really are going to the Fair?' cried Kevin. 'I must empty me money-box!'

His father laughed.

'I'm going to the Fair with the onions. Your mammy's coming to the Fair to watch out I make a good bargain. I'll need John to help push the cart, so he'll be there. Bridie was top in her class all last month and, anyway, I wouldn't leave her behind. But I thought mebbe you'd like to stay home and mind the babby, so yer grannie could have a treat.'

Kevin had taken his money-box down from the dresser. He stood with it in his hand trying not to look disappointed.

'Don't be tormentin the child,' chuckled the old grandmother. 'Sure, I'll be happy by the fire, wid the babby an me knitting. An I'll be lookin forward to hearin all the news when you do come back. I wouldn't want to be journeyin that distance. I've done it too often.'

Kevin took the thinnest of the knives and began to poke out his money.

He had been saving for so long he thought he must have a fortune.

'I'll be able to buy everything at the Fair!' he thought proudly, and began to think of the presents he would bring back home.

But the money-box didn't feel very heavy and when he shook it the rattle didn't sound nearly full.

'Silver takes less room than pennies,' he comforted himself.

He had all his presents planned. He smiled as he looked over at Bridie carefully folding the pink frock. Bridie made all her presents herself, so did John. Kevin stopped poking out pennies to wonder what Bridie had made for him. He had tried to find out. But she wouldn't tell and though he had searched every corner of the cabin he hadn't been able to discover where her presents were hidden.

She looked over at Kevin now with laughing eyes as though she guessed what was puzzling her brother.

At last his green post office was empty – sixteen pennies, one sixpenny piece, three threepennies and four halfpennies. Kevin counted them up – two-and-sixpence.

'I thought I had heaps more!' he told himself. 'Heaps!'

But his mother was serving out the fish, while John cut the bread and Bridie laid the table.

As he ate Kevin wished he were a clever carpenter like John. But though he could sing all the ballads in the twopenny song-sheet and had every poem in the school reader off by heart, Kevin was clumsy with his hands. Yet his father did say he'd be a great gardener when he grew up if he'd only remember to push the spade into the ground and not forget to take it out again.

At last they were on the road. Sure enough, the rain had stopped and great tattered clouds were sweeping out to sea. There was a strange white light over the mountains and, as Kevin stared, the moon rose in the sky.

There weren't many people on the road when they started: a few fishermen from the Head and a man belonging to a mountain farm leading a donkeycart with his wife and baby sitting in the front, and four bonhams lying at the back on a comfortable bed of straw.

'Isn't it well to be them!' exclaimed Mr Hanlon. 'Will you look at them, riding to the Fair like gentry, while we have to wear out our shoe leather!'

He pushed the handcart piled with large, brown onions, and Bridie, who always liked to be with him, danced alongside, her fair hair floating from under her red tammy and her muffler twisted round and round her neck so that she had to hold her head high. John walked with his mother, carrying the basket of thyme, sage and rosemary. The fragrant smell was blown beyond them to

Kevin. He had started ahead of the others but there was so much to look at that gradually he had dropped back, until he trudged alone, his hands in his pockets.

The road was white and glistening. Shadows of trees and rocks lay across it, black and still. The shadows of those who followed the road kept with them, so that in some places the way seemed crowded.

Far ahead the lights of Lismoyle twinkled in rows and patches. A great blaze of light rose from the centre, and Kevin knew that showed the market-place where the greatest Fair of the year was being held.

When Kevin wasn't thinking of the poems he had learned he did sums in his head. This night he needed all the arithmetic he knew to stretch half-a-crown as far as he wanted it to go.

'I want six presents!' he said. 'Two-and-six is thirty pennies. That's fivepence each. Now how can I buy a doll or a mouth-organ or a ball or a pipe or any kind of a present at all for only fivepence? Wish I could make things. Wish I could be clever like Bridie and John!'

For all his adding up Kevin saw everything about him – the beehive huts where people had lived long, long years ago, the little paths up mountains, the sea-wall and the waves, not so high or rough as they had been all day, but tumbling and tossing in a friendly, comfortable way.

He watched the shadows too, but the moonlight was strange and confusing so that he could not tell which were shadows and which people. As Mr Hanlon and Bridie passed the old fort, older even than the huts, one shadow grew longer and longer until it reached where Kevin stood.

Suddenly the shadow was gone, but a tall, thin man, wearing a black coat down to his heels and with a wide-brimmed hat pulled over his eyes, walked beside the boy, singing to himself.

On his back he carried a creel, beautifully made of green rushes. It had a lid so finely woven Kevin envied the one who had made it.

Kevin liked ballad singers and all wanderers. But most of all he liked pedlars.

He was startled but not frightened by the stranger, for the bright eyes peering at him from under the broad brim of the hat were friendly. The man was singing so softly Kevin had to listen carefully to make out the words:

> 'If you meet the Shadow Pedlar
> On the road from home to market,
> With his pack
> On his back,
> He will buy your dreams:
> He will buy your dreams.'

'Are you the Shadow Pedlar?' asked Kevin.

'I am, indeed!' replied the man.

'Do you really buy dreams?'

The Pedlar nodded and hummed the tune of his song. It was gay and friendly, and strange too.

'What do you want them for?' persisted Kevin.

'I am the Sandman's brother,' said the Pedlar. 'You know the Sandman? He goes by at twilight with his sack and throws sand in your eyes to make you sleepy. But it's dream sand. You sleep, you dream. That's why he needs dreams. Most people dream only at night. Some don't dream at all. A few dream all the time. They can spare dreams for the others. I buy them for me brother. I should be called the Dream Pedlar – if I had me rights!'

Kevin wasn't sure if he understood.

'That's a gorgeous creel,' he said politely.

'There's better inside,' replied the Pedlar.

His voice was so faint it was like a distant whisper. But now Kevin could hear him easily.

'Could I see what's inside?' he asked.

'What do creels hold?' demanded the stranger harshly, yet still his voice was faint and distant.

Kevin put his head on one side.

'Turf, or onions, or potatoes. Ah, sure, you can put anything in a creel.'

The man laughed.

'You don't expect to see turf or onions or potatoes when I lift the lid, do you, Kevin?'

The boy shook his head. He wondered how the man knew his name.

'There'll be no turf or onions or potatoes in that creel, I know well!' he said eagerly.

The Pedlar stepped to the low sea-wall and letting the creel rest there, flung back the lid.

'All you can see is yours! The others didn't see me or me basket, and if they had looked inside they'd have seen only seaweed and cockle-shells.'

Kevin gasped with delight.

'The presents!' he cried. 'The wonderful presents!'

The Pedlar sang softly as he picked out a sleeping doll and laid it gently on the wall. Beside it he put a white-and-green rattle with a satin ribbon tied to it. Then came a polished pipe of ruddy wood and a tiny box, which the Pedlar flicked open with one finger and showed Kevin little tools that might have been made for a leprechaun. The boy gazed after his brother, thinking how delighted John would be. The pair of scissors grannie had longed for, and the silver thimble he had wanted for his mother were there too.

The Pedlar began to wrap them in yards and yards of green, red and yellow tissue paper. Then he made a parcel of brown paper tied with red string.

'Is there anything else you're after wanting?' he asked, as he tied the last knot and laid the parcel in Kevin's arms.

'But I've only two-and-six!' stammered the boy, hugging the parcel. 'I should have told you.'

'Listen!' said the Shadow Pedlar. 'Listen to me now! You were dreaming and you bringing in the turf. You were dreaming as you took the pennies and the sixpence and the threepenny pieces, not to mention the four halfpennies, out of the money-box. You're always dreaming – sleeping and waking. And you never hide your dreams, you give them out. Did no one ever tell you, Kevin, that dreams are the most important things in the world?'

He began to sing:

'You have met the Shadow Pedlar
Going to the Christmas Fair,
With his pack
On his back.
He has bought your dreams:
He has bought your dreams.'

Then he whistled a tune like a blackbird.

'Was there anything you were wanting to ask me, lad?' he demanded.

Kevin was ashamed of his curiosity. But what harm could there be in knowing?

'I wish I knew what Bridie·made for me and where she's hidden it?' he muttered.

The Pedlar laughed.

'Sure, I couldn't let Bridie down, she's the only one could tell you that!'

He swung the creel over his shoulder by the strap and set off along the road. The others were far ahead, but his legs were so long Kevin had to run to keep up with him.

They were coming near the town, over the bridge, by the canal. There were lights in the houses and a gust of noise became loud, dropped, grew loud again. Kevin tried to make out one sound from another – men shouting, dogs barking, a drum beaten to the time of a march. Someone was singing – that was the Pedlar at his side. He could hear the lowing of cows, the plaintive unceasing cries of sheep. A defiant cock crowed loudly and a trumpet answered him.

'It's the Fair!' shouted Kevin, turning to the Pedlar.

There were people coming up from the houses along the bay, from farms up the river, from cabins hidden by their own turf piles – more people than Kevin remembered seeing before. But the Pedlar had disappeared.

Kevin looked at the shadows. There were too many people on the road to leave space for all their shadows. But beyond the road, on the marshy fields, the telegraph poles, the electric standards, cast the shadows of giants.

'Kevin!' called his mother. 'Where are you?'

'Kevin!' shouted his father. 'Do you hear me?'

'Kev-in! Kev-in! Kev-in!' sang John and Bridie laughing at themselves.

They were waiting under the line of trees. Kevin ran towards them and they went on – afraid of being late. Noise, lights, confusion, made the town important and happy, and Kevin was excited, though even when he caught up, he kept behind the others. He didn't want them to see the presents yet.

They joined the stream of people flowing to the old market. Mr Hanlon sold his onions to Donal Heggarty who kept the vegetable shop at the corner of the lane. Donal bought the bunches of herbs too.

'Thanks be! Now we've nothing to do but enjoy ourselves and spend the money!' declared Mr Hanlon, slapping his hands together, for he had made a good sale.

Kevin carried the basket and slipped his parcel inside. Soon it was covered with apples and oranges, a bag of mixed biscuits and a string of sausages. A man was tossing six plates in the air, tipping each as it came down, sending it up again, so that the six were all moving at the same time. The three children stood watching while their father and mother went off to buy the bacon and candles, the cheese, tea, sugar, all the marketing for Christmas. When they came back the handcart looked full, but Mr Hanlon took the basket and easily found room for it.

'Donal will lave us stow the cart behind the shop till we're on our way back,' he said.

Kevin hated being parted from his presents, but the basket was heavy!

He forgot presents and Pedlar until they were listening to a ballad singer who was singing *Kelly, the Boy from Killann*. Then Kevin thought he heard a clear voice with the sweetness of a flute joining in. But no-one else noticed. They threw rings and Bridie won a green glass tumbler. They saw a strong man who could lift a big boy in each hand, and a girl who danced on a bread-board without once going over the edge.

At the corner of the market a forest of small Christmas trees blocked the pavement and, as he squeezed after the others, Kevin was sure the Pedlar was there, tossing handfuls of frost over the green branches. When he looked again it was only a shadow and the light from a big street lamp meeting the moonlight.

Close by the crates of fowl and geese a woman was making tea in a big kettle over a turf fire.

'I could do with a cup of tea!' sighed Mrs Hanlon.

Mr Hanlon felt in his pockets.

'The last penny is gone!' he declared. 'Didn't I

feel it in me bones we shouldn't have bought the nuts!'

'Oh, Daddy, there's barm bracks to eat with the tea! We must have some!' coaxed Bridie.

'And ham sandwiches!' added John.

Wasn't Kevin proud when he put his hand in his pocket and pulled out his money – the whole two-and-six!

'There's all the money we want!' he said.

'You saved that for presents, child!' his mother reminded him.

'I have them all. They're in the basket!' he told her, sliding onto the long form behind the table with the white cloth and the flowered cups and saucers.

The tea was hot, strong and sweet. The barm brack was rich with spice and raisins, and spread with yellow butter. Kevin gazed at the Fair and wished they could stay till morning.

The people were dancing. The horses and cows and sheep were dancing. Kevin's head nodded; his eyes closed; he was asleep.

He woke to find himself riding in the handcart. The bacon and parcels were stacked at one side. Bridie was beside him wrapped in the old shawl. John and his father were pushing the cart and his mother walked beside it, carrying the basket, her hand on Bridie's shoulder.

The moon still shone, but now it was overhead.

Even brighter to Kevin was the golden glow of the candle in the window welcoming them home.

'That was a grand dream I had,' he thought, remembering the Shadow Pedlar.

Was it a dream? Were those lovely presents only part of a dream?

Bridie stirred and opened her eyes. She looked at Kevin's puzzled face.

'I knitted you a gorgeous belt, Kevin,' she murmured. 'All the colours of the rainbow. It's at the bottom of grannie's box!'

Kevin rubbed his eyes, scrambled to the ground and took the basket from his mother.

'Let me carry it, Mammy,' he said. 'I'll be the first home!'

He raced ahead, the frost crunching under his feet as good as snow. He couldn't be sure if he had been dreaming.

He pushed open the door. The baby was asleep in her cradle. Grannie slept on the settle. The fire glowed red and the candle-light was reflected in the holy pictures on the walls and glittered on the green leaves and red berries of the holly.

'I'd be terrible glad if those presents are real!' thought Kevin.

He put the basket on the table and took out the apples and oranges, the biscuits and the sausages. There the brown-paper parcel and, as he untied the red string, he heard the wheels of the cart grate on the stones before the house, while away up the road a voice was singing:

> 'Kevin met the Shadow Pedlar
> On the road from home to market,
> With his pack
> On his back.
> And he bought his dreams.
> And he bought his dreams.'

THE FAIRY FORT OF SHEEN

from *Brogeen Follows
the Magic Tune* (1952)

*Brogeen the leprechaun is shoemaker to the
fairies and lives for most of the time in the
Fairy Fort of Sheen. The fort is a special un-
derground cavern, crowned on the surface
by a tell-tale ring of stones. Sometimes Brogeen, who is very adventurous, becomes
restless and – unlike the other fairies and
leprechauns – sets off on his travels to the
outside world, where he usually finds that
his meetings with humans bring all sorts of
trouble.*

Since he could remember, Brogeen had lived in
the High Fort of Sheen, where the Slieve Mish
Mountains rise from the sea.

A stranger would notice only a ring of steep
rocks with very green grass growing between.
Brogeen knew where the big door, and dozens of
little ones, opened upon the fort crowded with the
Good People.

There were always visitors from other forts. Day
and night the place was gay with music, dancing
and feasting; busy with work and excited by news
from all over the country.

Everyone in Sheen had a gift: the Queen – beauty, the King – courage, the Chief Harper – the gift of music. Some could cook, some embroider. One little fellow made all who looked at him happy with a glance from his laughing eyes. Brogeen had the gift of shoemaking, for he was a leprechaun.

The Master Craftsman, who journeys through the country teaching and encouraging good work, had once praised Brogeen. He had stayed one night in the fort but for days after even the tiniest apprentices tried to work harder and with greater skill.

But Brogeen was the only one he had praised.

There were other leprechauns in the fort, yet Brogeen was the cleverest of them all. That was why Brogeen was kept far busier than he wished.

Brogeen was proud of his gift, but when he should have been finishing a pair of shoes for the Queen, he'd be helping the Chief Harper tighten his strings, or smoothing the floor for a dance, even trying to sing, though he had no more voice than a corncrake.

The Queen forgave him when she had to wear old shoes at the ball given to leprechauns, cluricauns, phoukas, banshees, glashans and the like when they came for the King's birthday. But when Brogeen forgot the laces for the high boots she intended to wear for the ride on Midsummer Night to Slieve na Mon, she was so angry even the King was afraid.

He liked Brogeen and began to make excuses.

'Sure, he's still young for a leprechaun,' he protested. 'He'll learn sense as he grows older.'

'By the time Brogeen learns sense I'll be too old to dance!' cried the Queen, tossing her head.

Her plaits were all loosened and the golden hair fell like a cloak around her.

'You'll never be too old to dance!' declared the King. 'And you'll always be the most beautiful woman in the whole of Ireland! Sure, Brogeen will have the laces ready before we set out!'

The Queen leaned back on her throne.

'Where is Brogeen?' she asked. 'Didn't you say we should start when the moon shows over Baurtigaun?'

The King anxiously poked his head out of the door. There was no sign of the moon but the light streaming from the fort showed whirling snowflakes and the mountains white and terrifying. The King shivered but he was too confused to notice the weather.

It was his business to remember the feasts and big days. He was clever and had a wonderful memory, though there were times when he was forgetful. Once he had them all decorating the big hall for Samhain (November Day) when they should have been preparing for Bealtaine (May Day).

Now, it did not occur to him that snowstorms

hardly ever arrived in Midsummer. Wrapping his velvet cloak about him, His Majesty strode through the fort shouting:

'Where is Brogeen? Where is Brogeen?'

The other leprechauns, and the tiny fellows who would be leprechauns one day, looked at each other.

'Did you see Brogeen?'

'I did not!'

'Wasn't he here a minute ago?'

'He was not!'

'I seen him helping you.'

'You did not!'

Up and down the big hall, in and out galleries and workshops, kitchens and music rooms, raged the King.

'Where is Brogeen? Where is Brogeen?'

A little smiling fellow came trotting round a corner.

'I seen Brogeen, Your Majesty! He was going on a message out of the fort and the storm raging round him.'

'Going on a message!' exclaimed the King scornfully. 'I might have known it. When Brogeen's wanted, he's always running after humans. Go off three of you and bring him back. And what's all this nonsense about a storm? There was no storm when I looked out.'

Three of Brogeen's friends ran out of the fort.

They sprang into the air and each time they began to drop towards the ground, sprang again. So it wasn't long before they were half-way to the village, and they went so fast the snowflakes hadn't a chance to cling to their clothes.

The wind blew against them and made each jump harder than the last. They were terribly fond of Brogeen, but they were beginning to wish he would give up his interest in humans and stay at home.

'One more jump and I'm finished!' gasped the smallest.

And then they heard Brogeen singing behind them. The snow had prevented them from seeing the fiddler and the leprechaun as they jumped in the air.

The three of them swung round. Now they could see Brogeen trotting before Batt Kelly and singing at the top of his voice. The wind sang louder so they couldn't hear the words of his song and they didn't bother. They were too terrified of fierce Batt Kelly.

'Come back home, Brogeen!' they called, clinging together and keeping at a safe distance from the fiddler, though he couldn't see or hear them. 'The King's looking for you. He's in a shocking great rage. The Queen wants her new bootlaces. Come back and find them.'

At last Brogeen heard. He knew he must go. Shaking his head mournfully, the leprechaun wondered how he could help Batt Kelly.

His three friends lost patience. They had no interest in strange fiddlers and their teeth were chattering with cold.

With a sudden pounce they caught hold of Brogeen, jumped into the air and carried him to the big door. There they shook off the snowflakes and bundled him inside.

'Don't let on you were colloughing with that fiddler!' they advised. 'Just pretend you didn't know you were wanted.'

'Whisha! Tis cold out there!' said Brogeen, shivering. 'But snow is wonderful. You don't know what you're missing, staying inside here.'

By this time the King had discovered that Midsummer wouldn't be with them for many nights and days. A storm was raging in the world outside. Only banshees and that foolish Brogeen were abroad.

'It's extraordinary how I could make such a mistake!' he thought. 'Wouldn't you think someone would have mentioned it. Even the Queen should know we don't have Midsummer in the middle of winter! I do hope she doesn't discover what a muddle I'm in!'

'What need is there to ride all the way to Slieve na Mon for a bit of a dance?' he said out loud. 'Can't we dance here in peace and comfort? Where are the musicians? What are the cooks doing? The

Queen's starving and so am I!'

'If you please, Your Majesty,' said a very meek voice behind him, 'I have the Queen's bootlaces safe in me bag and here they are – golden, soft, fine, the best I ever made!'

The King glared over his shoulder.

'What would Her Majesty be wanting with bootlaces when she's not going riding but will be dancing here? Off with you! Bring her the new silver shoes that you made so well.'

Delighted at escaping so easily, Brogeen was darting away when the King remembered all the fuss he had been making.

'You'll have to be punished for being such a nuisance,' he called. 'While we're all dancing you must take charge of the big door and see that no draughts come in.'

He marched away and Brogeen hugged himself for he had never been allowed to take charge of the door before.

The regular Keeper of the Door was furious. He scowled at Brogeen.

'I'll not budge from here till me supper's ready!' he growled. 'Let you tell them to put me supper on the table, so I won't be kept waiting a minute. I have me rights!'

Brogeen took a last peep at the stormy world outside and there, towering above him, was the quarrelsome fiddler.

WITHOUT NUALA

from *Delia Daly of Galloping Green* (1953)

Mr and Mrs Daly own a flower and fruit shop in the village of Dunooka in Co. Cork. They have two sons, Dominick and Hugh Patrick, and two daughters, Delia and Nuala. Delia is the younger of the girls and there is a good deal of sisterly rivalry between them, although they are good friends. When their mother's wealthy Cousin Kate offers to pay for one of the girls to go to boarding school in Dublin, Delia feels that she will be the first choice. But she is not at home when Cousin Kate comes to make the arrangements and Nuala is chosen instead.

When Delia went up to bed that first night after Nuala left home, she climbed the stairs on tiptoe. They were dark but the bedroom was bright with moonlight.

As she closed the door of the living-room, her mother's voice followed her,

'I never knew a house full of people could be so empty.'

'That's the way I feel!' thought Delia. 'I wonder what Nuala is doing now! Will she be going to bed? Has she made a friend? Is she happy, or does she want to be here with me? Oh, how I wish I'd come back in time that day Cousin Kate was here! I'd be in Dublin now!'

Delia stared out of the open window, gazed at the silver path across the waves, watched the lighthouse and a steamer with blazing portholes going on to Cork, yet saw none of them. She listened to the booming of the sea below but without hearing.

Slowly, as if walking in her sleep, she crossed the room, knelt before the little chest of drawers, pulled at the bottom one and, groping under her clean clothes, drew out her doll, Finovar.

Cousin Kate had sent it from France and at once Delia wanted to call it Nuala. It had golden curls, blue eyes which opened and shut and three dimples. But Nuala refused.

'How silly to want two Nualas in the one house!' she said.

'Call the doll Finovar!' suggested grandfather. 'She was a lovely princess, daughter of the Warrior Queen, Maeve!'

So the doll was called Finovar.

Delia settled her against Nuala's pillow.

'I'll tell you the stories I used to tell Nuala,' she said. 'Once upon a time –'

She stopped.

'I wish I knew what Nuala is doing now,' thought Delia.

But the doll was company when she opened her eyes and saw the golden head gleaming in the morning light.

It was strange to have two chairs for her clothes and no one to race with, washing and dressing.

A gull perched on the window-sill and looked in at her with its bold, clear eye and its head on one side.

'You can stare,' said Delia. 'There's only one of me, and Nuala's away in Dublin, where I should be!'

The bird opened its beak as if yawning.

'If I had wings like yours I'd fly up there and say hallo!'

The wings spread, showing the soft white underfeathers, and the gull darted away across the cove, to its nest on Phouka cliff.

Everyone was very kind to Delia at breakfast and her mother only smiled when she settled her doll in Nuala's seat.

'I thought Finovar would remind us,' she said.

When she came through the shop on her way to school Rory Egan was outside, sitting on the sea-wall.

'Like to ride with me?' he asked. 'Where's Dom?'

She shook her head.

'I don't know! He always bolts his breakfast and runs off.'

Rory showed her how to stand at the back of his bicycle. They could ride only through the village, for the school was perched beside the chapel on top of Lissaphouka Hill and the bicycle had to be pushed all the way.

Delia was glad not to be alone. Since her first day at school she had always been with Nuala and now it was hard not to say: 'Look, Nuala! Do you know your lesson, Nuala?'

Rory told her about the table he was helping his uncle to make and how the doll's house they had finished last week was on show at the big toyshop in Youghal. He didn't ask questions and, when they reached the school gate, without a word he went towards the boys' entrance and left her with Miss Marcella.

'You'll be lonesome without your sister,' said the teacher. 'So I've changed your seat over to the window. You'll have something to look at there. Una Caffrey doesn't mind.'

Una Caffrey was the top girl and her seat was the best. The others moved up so that Nuala's absence left no gap.

For a little while, looking across the road and down upon the roofs of Dunooka, Delia forgot Nuala. But when Una paused in answering a question and Delia prompted her in a whisper, the older girl's shocked face made her remember.

'If Nuala had stayed, I'd still be in that horrid

seat with nothing to look at,' she thought. 'No, I wouldn't; I'd be in Dublin!'

During lunch-time she sat on the bank with Una. It made her feel grand and generous to share an apple and her ham sandwiches. Una had only a thick wedge of plain soda bread, heavy and damp. She broke it in two and Delia pretended to eat her piece, but she crumbled it and scattered the bits for the birds.

Una boasted how she would go to England when she was sixteen and send home enough money to buy her mother a new shawl and her father a pair of boots.

When school was over, there was Rory leaning on his bike and flicking away the dust with a big dock leaf.

'Hold tight!' he said, as she ran over, delighted to be saved the long trudge down hill.

It seemed to Delia that she and Rory were falling. The road rushed up to meet them, then passed on. He knew by her clutch on his shoulder that she was frightened. He hoped her foot wouldn't slip, but he didn't say a word, neither did Delia.

'One time I'll teach you to ride properly,' he promised, as they stopped at the shop.

'Daddy!' she cried, darting through the doorway. 'I rode all the way home on Rory's bike! Won't Nuala be surprised when I write and tell her?'

She turned to her mother.

'Did you see me?' she asked.

'I did!' replied Mrs Daly. 'And I'm not sure if it's safe at all for a girl to be perched at the back of a lad's bike.'

'Rory is very careful,' said Mr Daly. 'Delia'd be safe enough with him.'

'We passed everybody!' cried Delia. 'It was better than flying, or maybe it was nearly as good!'

'Look at poor Dom!' grumbled Mrs Daly. 'I've been watching that long stretch of Lissaphouka Hill and that boy staggering down in the heat and dust. Rory Egan's never thought of giving him a lift!'

'Sure the old bike wouldn't stand it,' explained Mr Daly. 'The uncle bought it for Rory from a travelling junk dealer for ten shillings. Dom's a hardy lump of a lad, while little Delia weighs no more than a fly.'

Delia didn't wait to hear them. She danced out to the garden at the back, where Mr Mangan from Cloneynoggins was showing her grandfather an old book he had bought at an auction.

'Grandfather! Rory Egan brought me home on his bike. I stood up at the back and it was like being a seagull!'

She inhaled the musty odour of the yellowed pages her grandfather was turning very gently. With it was mingled the pungent smell of sun-baked seaweed, the scent of lavender and thyme.

Mr Mangan started, frowned at the interruption, then met her sparkling eyes.

'I might feel that way meself if I'd found the first manuscript ever written in Ireland,' he chuckled. 'But I must be on my way to me brother's. They'll be waiting tea for me.' He was smiling at her and she smiled back.

'I hope you will find that manuscript,' said Delia, 'unless grandfather wants it.'

She heard Dominick chatting in the kitchen and ran in to tell him of her achievement.

'I saw you!' he said. 'And the old bike smothered me with dust! Little you cared!'

But nothing could cloud her happiness until she realized that he was joking to cheer her loneliness. Then she missed Nuala again.

After tea they sat on the steps Mr Daly had made down the sloping cliff. The garden dropped in terraces to the edge, where a low wall broke the wind.

'I'm walking over to Cloneynoggin and Mr Mangan's brother will drive me back,' said grandfather. 'If Delia'd like to come, twould be a change for her.'

Mrs Daly stared at him in amazement. Never before had he asked one of them to go walking or driving.

'I'd love to come!' gasped Delia, as astonished as the rest.

She went off with the old man, hand in hand, he flourishing his stick, Delia dancing beside him. She looked up and he looked down.

Mr and Mrs Daly, gazing after them, wondered what they could be talking about.

'Legends!' decided Mr Daly. 'He'll be telling her legends. Delia'll like that!'

'How could a child like Delia understand legends?' demanded Mrs Daly. 'Now if it was Dom!'

Delia and her grandfather climbed the stile at the far side of Galloping Green and took the path which skirted Lissaphouka Hill.

'Did you ever hear of *The Three Sorrows of Story-telling*?' asked Mr Burke.

Delia sighed.

'Grandfather! Don't tell me a sad story, or I'll be thinking of how Nuala is away by herself up in Dublin and I'm down here alone.'

'You're not alone!' said the old man firmly. 'And Nuala isn't by herself up in Dublin. She's having the chance you longed for and Dominick needs. Maybe you'll both have it yet. Nuala should be glad and happy. If she isn't, sure she's young. So no more nonsense!'

'No, grandfather!' said Delia, very meekly.

The old man smiled at her.

'There is sorrow in the world, Delia, and we

must face it. But when it's beautiful sorrow, and grand sorrow, all we can ask for is the courage to meet it. Now, will I tell you the story of Nuala, daughter of Lir, who was turned into a swan, or would you sooner we sang a bit of a marching song to shorten the road?'

Delia swung round in front of him.

'A story about Nuala! Oh, grandfather! Begin at once, or we'll be at the Mangans' before you've finished.'

Matt Kearney was out after rabbits when he saw them. He lay down behind a clump of bracken. Though he didn't mind Delia seeing him, he wasn't so sure of old Mr Burke. He told his wife about it when he reached home, loaded down with provisions for the pot.

'The poor slip was cryin her heart out an, thinks I, the old gentleman's scoldin the girleen an if he doesn't let up I'll peg a stone at him. Then if the young one didn't choke an cry out: "Go on, grandfather! Go on! What happened next?" So I kep very still an quiet till they passed on. Sure the old fella was just tellin a story to keep her mind off her troubles.'

'He's a gran old man, a gentleman!' declared Mrs Kearney. 'Only yesterday when Der axed him for a penny to buy Peggy's Leg, he gave the child sixpence an another to Bernie, who never axes anyone for anythin, God help her!'

'He's a gentleman, if ever there was one!' mumbled Matt, his mouth filled with bread and cheese and strong tea.

'Rale old stock!' agreed Mrs Kearney.

The story of the Children of Lir lasted until Delia and her grandfather reached the gate of the Mangans' house at the end of a boreen so neat and crowded with flowers, it was the talk of the district.

'That's one of *The Three Sorrows of Story-telling*,' said the old man.

'When will you tell me another?' asked Delia, rubbing her face dry with her clean pocket handkerchief.

But Mr Burke was opening the gate and the Mangans were coming out to meet them, so she wasn't answered that time.

Mrs Mangan had been in America where she learned to make doughnuts. After eating six brown sugary ones and drinking two cups of coffee, Delia was thankful they hadn't to walk home, but were to drive back in style.

Besides making doughnuts, Mrs Mangan was a wonderful comforter.

'Think of all Nuala will have to tell you when she's home for Christmas!' she said. 'Why, child! I cried me eyes out when we had to send the three boys away to school. Now I'm looking forward so to their letters and the holidays, I hardly know they're

gone before they're home again. And sure, you'll
be going up to Dublin yourself one day.'

'Nuala doesn't write very good letters,' said
Delia.

'Then you must write very good ones to make
up!' Mrs Mangan told her.

The carnival was a great help to Delia. She went
on the swings and hobby-horses every day and
Dominick didn't once mention Dublin.

The last day there was a great raffle and Delia
had the winning ticket. Everyone laughed when
she chose a huge aluminium saucepan, but her
mother was so pleased Delia was glad she had
resisted a fountain-pen.

'Though to be sure an iron one would have
been more sensible,' said Mrs Daly. 'Still, twas
very thoughtful of you, Delia! You're getting to be
a great help to me, now poor Nuala's away from
us.'

So it was not until night-time that Delia really
thought of Nuala. Then there was the doll, Finovar,
listening without interrupting or asking questions.
But she couldn't make Delia laugh, or sing the
songs she liked best.

A letter came from Nuala, not a long one, but
the longest she had ever written, for there had only
been the Christmas and Easter school letters
before. She was well and it was a grand school. She
was learning French and singing, and she would try

to work hard. She sent her love and would write once a week on Sunday.

'I wish she'd told us a bit more,' said Mrs Daly.

'It's a letter!' declared Mr Daly.

After that Nuala didn't seem so far away.

IF I WERE A BLACKBIRD

from *Tinker Boy* (1955)

Tessa Nolan lives in the village of Danesford with her parents and her brothers, Michael Joe and Derry. One day some travelling tinkers come with their carts and tents to settle for a while on Black Boar Common outside the village. The villagers do not welcome them as they do not like to mix with tinkers, but Tessa takes no notice of their talk. One morning on the way to school she meets a tall, dark tinker boy called Dara McDara, who is walking the road to school with his mother. Tessa agrees to bring him to school with her but when they join the class the other children are rude and unfair to the new pupil.

The teacher was writing in the Attendance Book but looked up as Tessa came in.

'One day you may be here first,' she said, 'but I doubt it.'

Tessa smiled nervously.

'I am glad I'm not late, Miss MacDermot,' she stammered. 'This is Dara MacDara with me. His mother sent him.'

Everyone stared with interest as they heard the

grand sounding name. When Tessa moved to one side and Dara, barefoot, in tattered clothes, his dark hair rumpled, stepped forward, the teacher looked scornful and the scholars giggled.

The boy gazed from face to face. One by one each looked away. Michael Joe, who was sitting in front, his brother beside him, nudged Derry.

'Isn't that Tessa all over!' he muttered. 'Always making a show of herself!'

Derry grinned at his sister.

'Poor Tessa!' he thought. 'She is a duffer!'

'What book are you in?' Miss MacDermot asked the tinker boy.

He shook his head.

'Never been to school before!' he explained.

The teacher was startled.

'Then you can't read!' she said sharply.

'Course I can read!' retorted Dara. 'School isn't the only place for learning!'

'Indeed?'

And Miss MacDermot's smile was even more scornful than usual.

'We shall be able to judge your great learning later on,' she added.

Another giggle rippled round the school. Dara's dark face flushed. Tessa, the meekest girl in Ferry Bank School, indeed in all Danesford, found herself growing angry.

'It isn't fair!' she thought. 'They are mean!'

'What is your age, Dara MacDara?' asked Miss MacDermot.

'Twelve last month!' the boy told her.

While she entered his name in the book he looked about him.

Ferry Bank School was old and small. The windows were high up, the rafters and walls discoloured with smoke. But Dara saw the maps, the open cupboard, its shelves crowded with books, the blackboard half-covered with chalk figures and resolved to learn all he could, to show these gigglers he was better than any of them, to be a credit to the name of MacDara.

'Sit there!' said the teacher, pointing to an empty place beside Michael Joe.

'I'm not going to have a tinker sit beside me!' declared Michael Joe, moving along so that there was no room on the seat.

The other children, even the little ones, followed his example and spread out.

'Dara can sit with me! There's heaps of room!' said Tessa loudly.

'That might be best,' Miss MacDermot told her.

Because she was so tall, Tessa sat at the back, under the picture of Saint Patrick, in a corner beside the recess where the coats hung. By squeezing, two could sit there and Dara followed her up the room as proudly as though she were sharing the best seat in the school with him.

Tessa had a new exercise book in her bag and gave him that. Her old one still had several blank pages. She pushed a pen towards him and sucked her pencil hoping it might write thickly enough to be mistaken for ink.

Prayers gave them all a chance to settle down. The first lesson was arithmetic. Miss MacDermot wrote a sum on the board. Tessa was tired of saying: 'Teacher! The board shines!' and had reconciled herself to being punished for mistakes made because she couldn't see the figures.

'The board always shines,' she murmured, sorry for her companion because she thought he would suffer as she did.

But Dara's eyes were accustomed to seeing far more difficult things than figures on a gleaming blackboard. He wrote down the sum in thick, bold figures. He didn't know what to do with them but watched Tessa as she copied from him and triumphantly worked out the problem. Frowning, he imitated her. Then the two of them sat back, contentedly waiting for the slower scholars.

Michael Joe collected the exercise books.

'Two dunces!' he said jeeringly as he took theirs.

'Eejit!' retorted Dara.

'You wait!' Michael Joe warned him.

At first Dara didn't understand the mental arithmetic and Tessa, who was almost as good at figures as her father, whispered the answers to him. Soon he was answering almost before Miss MacDermot had finished speaking. She looked at him thoughtfully, wondering at his quickness.

The last lesson of the morning was singing and the song they were learning was *The West's Awake*, a favourite with them all.

'We have ten minutes left,' said the teacher. 'Who will sing for us? Will you try, Tessa Nolan?'

Tessa had always refused. She was too shy. Dara gave her a nudge.

'*If I Were a Blackbird*,' he whispered. 'Start! I'll help you!'

She stood up and began at once:

'If I were a blackbird,
I'd whistle and sing –'

She remembered Dara's advice and sang at the top of her voice. After the first two lines the tinker boy's clear flute-like whistle joined in. Miss MacDermot sat with eyes wide open, scarcely understanding what was happening.

The boys and girls swung round in their seats and watched Tessa Nolan singing away as if she were the best singer at the annual Feis. Her brothers were puzzled. They had always laughed at Tessa's voice – it was so small and funny, coming from such a big girl. Now her singing and the tinker's whistling seemed to fill the shabby school.

Happy and confused, Tessa sat down. What had she done? Had she made a show of herself?

Derry, the brother who never teased, began to clap. The other children, delighted to make a noise, clapped and stamped too.

'Quiet, please!' said Miss MacDermot. 'You are free for an hour.'

The Nolans didn't go home for dinner. Mostly they brought sandwiches but today, because Mrs Cronin had been so late, the boys had a wedge of apple cake each. Tessa had forgotten to bring anything. When Dara saw some children running home and others settling themselves in sheltered corners to eat their packets of food, he turned to Tessa.

'Where's your piece?' he asked.

'I forgot to bring anything,' she told him. 'If I had some I'd share with you. But I don't mind!'

'Come with me,' said Dara. 'We'll find something!'

He darted from the schoolyard and Tessa closely followed him. Her brothers did not see her go. One moment she was there, the next she was gone. She seldom ate her lunch with them so they didn't bother.

Half-way across Black Boar Common, Tessa stopped.

'I daren't!' she thought. 'What would daddy say if he finds out? He doesn't like tinkers.'

Dara stopped too and turned round.

'What ails you?' he asked.

Tessa gazed at him speechlessly.

'Are you ashamed to eat with tinkers?'

He wasn't angry or mocking. Tessa could see that. He was wondering.

'I was only thinking,' she told him, and they went on together.

The camp was almost deserted, though a few fires still smouldered before the jumble of tents and carts, and some of the lean dogs were on guard.

Maura MacDara was there and saw them coming. She leaned over her half-door as if the caravan were a roadside cabin. Her eyes opened wide. Then she drew back to laugh unseen. She shook with laughter, yet not a sound came from her.

'Pon me word!' she muttered. 'Here's another taking a fancy to the tinkers' ways. Little did I know what I was starting! I like that young gerrul. Yet if her people heard she's consorting wid the likes of us, how would they take it? She's a dacent lassyo and I wouldn't want her to get a beating through the MacDaras!'

As the boy jumped up the steps and poked in his head she was stirring a round shining saucepan on the small stove.

'I've brought Tessa Nolan with me,' announced Dara.

'Sure, she's welcome!' answered his mother, rocking in a cushioned armchair which she filled tightly. 'Make yerself comfortable, girleen. Let ye dish out the food, Dara!'

'Mostly we take sandwiches,' explained Tessa. 'Only this morning we were in a muddle. The boys brought apple cake. I just forgot!'

'Then here's yer chance to try tinkers' stew,' chuckled Maura. 'Ye're lucky! The pot is fresh filled today and will serve the three of us twice over.'

Tessa sat just inside the door. Outside the caravan was as shabby as any cart in the camp, inside it was different. A seat ran along one side which at night opened into two beds with a partition between. A folded table was fastened opposite and above were lockers and shelves, one crowded with tattered books. At the end, near the driving seat, was the stove with saucepans and crockery piled around it. The place was untidy, the cushion covers torn and faded. Yet Tessa envied the MacDaras their home. She thought of driving into strange towns and out into the country again, of camping by the seashore and hearing the waves all night long. She wouldn't want to stay with the other tinkers. If this caravan were hers, she'd take it where the roads were empty and not a soul would know who she was.

'Ye didn't know tinkers lived this way?' asked Maura.

'I did not,' replied Tessa. 'It's better than a house. I like it more than a tent. You can go everywhere. You can travel all night and wake up in a different town each morning!'

'That was the way me poor husband, MacDara, used to talk,' said the tinker woman. 'He was better than a book. I could listen to him for hours. Twas he fixed this caravan up the way it is. Only he had it grand. I'm not one for sewing or painting. He could make anything he'd a mind to. Ah, he was the great little man!'

She filled three tin bowls with the hot stew and, as she slowly ate the first mouthful, Tessa knew she had never tasted such stew before.

She hadn't known she was so hungry. Neither Dara nor his mother talked while eating and the only sounds were the scraping of spoons, a sudden gulp, and Maura restlessly shifting her chair.

Tessa had emptied her bowl for the second time before she wondered what was in the stew.

'We never have stew like this at home!' she declared. 'What did you put in it? Maybe I could tell Mrs Cronin.'

'Was it good eating?' asked Maura.

'It was indeed!' declared Tessa.

'One day I'll teach ye to make it,' promised the

woman, laughing. 'One day when ye're a grown-up gerrul and run away from yer grand fine home to join the tinkers!'

'I'd never do that!' said Tessa quickly.

She felt frightened.

'There's many a one has,' said Maura. 'And never regretted!' she added thoughtfully.

She gave them each a mug of strong tea, sweetened with condensed milk, and a hard crust to dip in it.

'How did ye like the school, Dara?' she asked.

'There wasn't one would let me sit next to them, none but her!'

The boy nodded at Tessa.

Maura's face hardened. Her eyes filled with such anger the girl was startled.

'We sang,' she said, speaking very quickly. 'I mean I sang and Dara whistled – just like a black-bird! He's a grand whistler! I've never heard anyone like him. Neither had the others or Miss MacDermot. And they clapped, even Michael Joe clapped. Mrs MacDara! If Dara's as clever at other things as he is at whistling, every boy and girl in the school will be proud to sit next to him. I know they will!'

She was breathless as she finished speaking, her big brown eyes fixed anxiously on the indignant woman.

Maura rocked so quickly the tapping of the

chair was the sound of a dancer's feet. Gradually she slowed it down. The anger faded from her face and she smiled.

'Ye're a dacent crathure, Tessa Nolan!' she said. 'I've a real kindness for ye. I'll tell ye what I've told no other, only Dara himself. His father wasn't one of us. He was no tinker but a good tradesman, a carpenter of Danesford, before he turned away from his own people and joined us wanderers. That's why I want Dara to have the larning, all he can get of it! I don't want him to be a tinker. I want him to be like his father would have been, if he'd had good fortune.'

Maura sighed.

Tessa sat leaning forward, her elbows on her knees, her eyes were wide open and earnest, her long, straight yellow hair fell about her face.

In the distance a bell sounded.

'Time ye were on yer way to the school,' said the woman, as Dara spooned the last bit of tea-soaked bread in his mug and jumped out of the caravan.

'Thank you very much,' said Tessa politely, rising to follow him.

Maura drew her back.

'Ye'll always be welcome here, friendly child,' she said. 'But don't talk too much about us. Tisn't everyone would want their girl mixed up with tinker folk, not respectable people like the Nolans.'

Tessa wasn't sure if the woman was mocking her. She gazed quickly about the van, trying to remember everything there.

'I mayn't have the chance to come again,' she thought sadly.

Running down the steps, she went after Dara.

She turned once, to wave farewell, thinking Maura MacDara would be looking after them. But the door of the caravan was closed and there wasn't a sign of any living creature about the camp except the few grazing horses and the prowling dogs.

THE LIVERPOOL BOAT

from *The Bookshop on the Quay* (1956)

*Thirteen-year-old Shane Madden is an
orphan from Ballylicky, Co. Cork. After his
mother's death the boy lives on his Uncle
Joseph's farm but is not made to feel very
welcome. He is, however, very fond of his
Uncle Tim, a cattle drover. One day, when
Tim fails to return from a trip to Waterford,
Shane decides to run away and find him.
His travels take him to Dublin. Soon after
arriving in the city he makes friends with
the O'Clery family and their kind and
generous servant, Mrs Flanagan. Mr
O'Clery gives Shane a job in the family
business – the Four Masters' Bookshop. In
this extract he sets out once again to find
Uncle Tim. The O'Clery children want to
join him, but their mother insists they
remain and finish their homework.*

So Shane went alone. It was a straight line
along the dark quays, past the glittering lights
around O'Connell Bridge, beyond Butt Bridge and
the Customs House. Here, men with mongrel dogs
and bulging sacks sprawled on the wide steps.
Some were playing cards. Others gazed out on the

river and the ships anchored there, like men in a dream. One, a large garden fork across his knees, smoked a pipe comfortably and followed the passers-by with his quick, smiling eyes. His clothes were worn. He had a thick muffler round his neck and his shoes were sound. The other men were ragged. One had red toes poking through split boots.

The space behind the grand pillars sheltered them, but Shane knew how hard and cold stones grew at night.

'If it wasn't for the O'Clerys, I'd be like them!' thought the boy sympathetically.

On Rogerson's Quay, at the other side of the river, the cranes were still. Two little girls were dancing on the cobbles and a crowd watched their clever steps.

At first Shane walked quickly. But the nearer he came to the sheds where he could see big passenger steamers moored close in, the slower he went.

He passed one low down in the water. She looked very clean and proud, with her cream coat and the name *Lady Gwendoline* picked out in blue and brown. At the stern fluttered a blue flag with a golden harp and, on a lifebelt hanging by the bridge, 'Liverpool' was printed round it in thick black letters.

'If they tell me Uncle Tim went away on a boat,

should I follow him?' thought the boy. 'But how can I? Maybe I should wait! When I have the fare, I can make up me mind. All I have now is the shilling Mrs Flanagan lent me.'

Men, cases on their shoulders, trudged along the gutter. Girls, in twos and threes, carrying parcels and bags, hurried by, their high heels tapping. Taxis and lorries steamed along the roadway. Puddles gleamed. Straws and crumpled paper scurried before the wind. Overhead the lights shone steadily. Higher still, stars glittered in the dark sky. Men stumbled out from eating and drinking shops. Groups gathered at corners. Cries of 'Goodbye now!' 'We'll see you to the boat!' 'Don't forget your old friends!' 'Come back with a fortune!' 'Mind you write a long letter every week!' were tossed along the quays. Hootings and shouts and splashings rose from the river and the air throbbed.

Now the high, gloomy sheds rose, shutting out all sight of the ships. Between them were iron railings with closed gates, and Shane could hear the water lapping against the quay walls.

'Is this the way for the Liverpool boat that's going off tonight?' he asked every loiterer he passed. Not because he doubted it but because he wanted to hear the answer, 'Why wouldn't it be?' or 'Doesn't everyone know this is the place for the Liverpool boat?' 'Haven't ye two eyes in yer head? If ye can't see the ship itself by raison of the old sheds blocking the view, isn't that the Liverpool Bar over yonder? Up in the red lights! That tells ye!'

In the high wall were two narrow doors and here the passengers showed their tickets. Shane squeezed close to the man in charge at the steerage entrance.

'Do you be here every night when the Liverpool boat is going out?' asked Shane.

'I do indeed!' replied the man. 'If not me, then another! There's always one of us to guard the Liverpool boat.'

'Do you remember Tim Madden coming here? He's me uncle, a drover from West Cork.'

'That's a tough question, lad!' declared the man, never ceasing to look at tickets. 'A very tough question! There's only hundreds and hundreds raging along here night after night, with friends and neighbours, not to mention relations, come to see the last of them. That's all! And ye expect me to remember a West Cork drover! Haven't I something better to be doing with me time and me interests?'

'He's tall and thin!' persisted Shane. 'He has red hair and blue eyes. He can sing and whistle better than anyone else and he's the finest drover in all Cork. He can do anything with animals!'

'So that's his name, is it!' cried the man indignantly. 'Tim Madden, the impudent scoundrel! Well I remember him, and if I see him again I'll have a few words with that same boyo! When ye find him, ye can tell him I'm here, waiting!'

'Did he go away on the boat?' asked Shane, pressing close to the fence, for passengers and their luggage were crowding through.

'If I knew that, I'd be wiser than I am!' said the man bitterly. 'It was the busiest night of the year and before I could stop him a red-headed lad that might be your uncle, for the other chap was calling him his "darling Tim", dashed through and nearly flattened me. I saw one ticket and one ticket only! Sure they wouldn't let him on board without one, and if they did he wouldn't be let land the other side!'

'Didn't you see him again?' asked Shane.

'I did not and what's more I don't want to! Off with you now! If I set eyes on that long, lanky drover again he'll not pass me if he has twenty tickets! If you want to see the *Munster* going down the river, get along there!'

A sudden piercing blast sent Shane running. He had imagined he would see emigrants swarming up crowded gangways and the ship sinking lower and lower as each one stepped on deck, but the high shed had hidden all that.

He followed others, hurrying over a narrow bridge and out on to an open part of the quay. Now

he could see the *Munster*, a light low down on its mast, a huge funnel and rows of white faces turned towards the crowd. He listened to the cries of farewell, the promises to write the good wishes. The sounds were confused. If Uncle Tim had been there his voice would have been caught up in the general tumult, his face a white oval.

The ship was moving slowly past them. Now it swung out to the centre of the river. The rows of faces were hidden by a forest of waving hands and handkerchiefs. Shane pulled off his scarf and waved that. The lights were growing dimmer until only the red stern light could be seen as the boat steamed out into Dublin Bay.

Shane felt he was saying a long goodbye to Uncle Tim.

'Even if he hadn't a ticket, they might be easy on him!' thought the boy. 'No one but Uncle Joseph ever stood out against Tim Madden!'

The drizzle was turning to a downpour. There was no shelter unless he stood in a doorway and Shane was longing to be back in the Four Masters' Bookshop.

He reached O'Connell Bridge. The gay lights of O'Connell Street gleamed with a gentle shimmer through the rain. Beyond, lines of silver lights reached into the darkness.

'Dublin's a grand city,' he thought. 'It's almost as good as Cork!'

He crossed to Bachelors' Walk with the crowd, trying not to show his dread of the great buses, the stream of motors, the cyclists darting from unexpected directions like wasps.

There were fewer people here, so he began to run and came upon the bookshop before he expected it.

The outside books had been taken away but there were customers inside the lighted shop.

'Isn't it well for Mr O'Clery he has me now!' thought the boy. 'How will I begin?'

He put his cap and coat behind the door and went over to a man holding a book and staring hopelessly about.

'Can I help you, sir?' he asked.

He had served three people when Mr O'Clery looked out, saw Shane, and went on mending the spine of a heavy, leather-bound volume.

When the customers were gone Shane put the money he had taken in the drawer of the desk, in the corner behind a rampart of huge books, and stood looking into the big room. Mrs Flanagan's chair was drawn up to the fire. The O'Clerys sat round the table, bending over their tasks. He smiled as he watched them. He could go in and be welcomed. They'd want to know what had happened.

Bridgie looked up.

'Here's Shane back home!' she cried.

Then he stepped through the doorway.

WHAT KATHY FOUND

from *Jinny the Changeling* (1959)

For many years large numbers of Irish people had to emigrate to Britain to find seasonal employment. One of these, Conn Clery, has just left home in order to go to England for the harvesting. This means saying farewell for some months to his wife Josie and their children, Kathy and Phelim. Josie and the children have gone with him to the cross-roads, where he catches the lorry which will take him to the steamship in Belfast. Mrs McDermot and Mrs O'Reilly are two neighbours whose sons have also gone with Conn. The women and children are now all on the way home, not knowing that they are to have an encounter which will change their lives for ever. Traditionally, a changeling is a child left by the fairies in return for a human child which they have stolen.

For a few yards Kathy and Phelim walked very properly, hand in hand.

'Look!' cried Phelim suddenly.

He pulled his hand away from his sister's and ran to the side of the road. Scrambling up the bank he leaned on the stone wall.

Kathy joined him and they both gazed in delight at two donkeys, one grey and small who rolled on his back, his neat little hooves waving in the air; the other a tall, brown, gentle donkey, standing still and looking on in wonder at the other's antics.

'I'd sooner have a donkey than anything else in the world,' said Phelim, wondering why he had been so foolish as to ask his father to bring him a dog.

'I've never seen such a happy donkey before!' murmured Kathy, thinking of all the sad-eyed, forlorn little donkeys who had passed by the cabin.

'Come along, children!' came their mother's voice from the roadway. 'Kathy, run on like a good child, make up the fire and put on the kettle. I've never needed a cup of tea more!'

Kathy jumped down from the bank. The two women whose sons had gone with her father on the lorry were with her mother, so she went down the road without a word. Phelim straggled along behind her.

As she drew near the cross-roads she heard a plaintive cry.

'A kitten!' she thought. 'But where can it be?'

The cry came again. She was puzzled. It didn't seem quite like the noise a kitten would make.

She ran more quickly. Now she was at the cross-roads. Looking around her, up at the trees, down at the stream, she saw birds going in a leisurely way about their business. She heard quiverings of little unseen creatures in the grass. As her eyes rested on the tangled growth at the foot of the signpost she started and stood still, then stepped timidly across the road and gasped in wonder.

Her brother came up behind her.

'Why didn't you wait for me?' he grumbled.

Suddenly he became silent as he stood looking down with her.

'The doll he promised me!' said Kathy. 'Isn't daddy wonderful!'

Phelim nodded.

'Where's my dog?' he asked complainingly.

Kathy dropped to her knees in the long, tough, waving grass. A bramble caught at her frock but she did not notice.

An open, green rush basket lay half hidden in the grass. Snuggled into it was what Kathy had taken at first to be a doll. Now she saw it was a tiny baby. It opened its big brown eyes and gazed at her.

'A real live babby!' she said wonderingly.

'Mudder! Look what Kathy's found!' cried Phelim, running to the three women, clutching his mother's hand and coming back with them.

'A tinker's brat!' said Mrs McDermot contemptuously.

'The dote of a child!' exclaimed Mrs O'Reilly as Kathy pulled the baby from the basket and cuddled it in her arms.

'The poor wee thing!' sighed Mrs Clery. 'How could anyone leave it there, alone and uncared for!'

She took the baby from Kathy.

'Now, will ye see what it's wrapped up in? The finest lace I've ever set eyes on. And what's this?'

A piece of white paper was pinned to the baby's lace wrap. On it was written: *The name on me is Jinny. Take care of me.*

'What is it?' demanded Phelim, who was not very good at schooling. 'What is it?'

His mother told him.

'A lad your size should be able to read that for himself!' said Mrs McDermot severely.

'Good morra to yez,' said a hearty voice. 'What have ye found there? Is it a treasure trove?'

'It is indeed!' answered Mrs Clery, swinging round and smiling at the big policeman who had come up behind them and was dismounting from his bicycle.

'Pon me word!' he said, taking off his flat cap and wiping the inside of it, as well as his red shining face, with a handkerchief like a flag. 'That's a poor frightened scrap of a child. Whose is it?'

'Don't let him take it away!' cried Kathy. 'It's mine! I found it!'

She was going to explain how her father had promised her a doll that would walk and talk. In her own mind she was sure this wonderful baby was instead of that doll. But her mother's pale, gentle face warned her to keep silent.

'This is what the crathure was left in!' said Mrs McDermot. 'Tisn't often the tinkers leave their babbies behind.'

The policeman touched the baby's fair hair with the tip of his finger.

'That's no tinker's wee one!' he declared. 'And that bit of lace! Twas a rare worker crocheted that.'

Stooping, he lifted the green rush basket with his finger, held it up and whistled.

'I did a bit of plaiting rushes when I was a young lad!' he told his listeners. 'I was reckoned good, but I never did a job to equal that!'

The baby made a tiny sound like a bird.

'I haven't been long on this job,' said the young man. 'And I'm not rightly sure what I should be after doing.'

'You couldn't ride the bike and carry the babby too,' little Mrs O'Reilly told him. 'Twould be terrible if ye dropped that wee thing on the hard road!'

He rubbed his nose thoughtfully.

'I wonder if one of you women would take it in for the night until I find out the correct procedure?' he asked, looking appealingly from Mrs McDermot's scowling face to worried little Mrs

O'Reilly, and letting his eyes on Mrs Clery as she smiled down at the baby in her arms.

'I expect there's orphanages for the likes of these,' he said. 'And they're not too bad there, nowadays.'

Kathy was desperate.

'The babby's mine!' she cried. 'This is my Jinny instead of a doll. I want her!'

'Aren't you very bold!' said her mother.

But she was smiling, so Kathy didn't feel too anxious. She took the green rush basket the young policeman was holding out to her.

'So Jinny's her name, is it ?' he asked. 'Now, how did ye find that out?'

Mrs Clery showed him the writing on the strip of silky paper.

'*The name on me is Jinny,*' he read. '*Take care of me!*'

'The one who wrote that had good education!' he declared. 'Now I wonder who it was!'

The baby gave a tiny cry.

'The scrap's hungry,' said Mrs Clery. 'I'll take her home! You'll know where to find her!' she added.

She went off, Phelim at one side looking up at the baby, Kathy carrying the rush basket at the other.

The policeman, feeling very puzzled, mounted his bicycle and rode off. The two women standing at the cross-roads stared after the Clerys, then went their way, heads close together as they talked over what had happened.

'That woman has enough mouths to feed!' exclaimed Mrs McDermot. 'What right has she to add another to them ?'

'It's such a little mouth!' protested Mrs O'Reilly.

The Clerys' cabin looked very small and snug with the sunlight reflected from the windows, the flowers flaming in the garden and red roses flaunting themselves as high as the chimney-pot.

Mrs Clery had expected to return lonely and unhappy. Now she was sure Conn would come back safe and, though she knew she had scarcely enough money to buy food till the end of the month, she no longer worried. She'd manage somehow and – there'd be a letter.

Without being reminded, Kathy filled the kettle, Phelim brought in some sticks, and soon the baby was being fed with warm bread and milk, the teapot was brimming with good, strong tea, there was a dish of buttered toast in the middle of the table and a saucer filled with little chunks of cheese.

After tea Mrs Clery brought out the children's baby clothes she had folded away in one of the drawers.

'I gave most of them to poor wee ones that had

only rags to cover them,' she explained. 'But I made these myself and somehow I couldn't bear to part with them.'

'They're terrible pretty!' said Kathy, gazing at the tiny pink and blue and white garments.

'Honest! Did I really wear those doll's frocks?' asked Phelim in amazement, looking down at his short serge knickers and strong boots.

'You did wear them!' his mother assured him. 'And you looked so grand, people used to stop and talk to you!'

Phelim didn't know whether to be pleased or scornful.

'Baby talk, I suppose?' he asked.

'You know you were only a baby,' she told him, laughing. 'You wouldn't understand Greek or Latin!'

Mrs Clery gave Jinny a warm bath before the fire and Phelim blew bubbles to amuse her. She watched the rainbow-coloured balls go drifting off over the half-door and held out her hands as if wanting to follow them.

They dressed her in some of the tiny clothes Kathy had once worn, while the piece of lace she had been wrapped in was put in the top drawer of the big chest of drawers, where they kept other family treasures.

Inside was folded the piece of paper which had been fastened to it.

Mrs Clery sent Phelim to bring out the little cart Conn Clery had made when the boy was no bigger than Jinny. With a pillow and a soft blue shawl, the baby had a grand bed, as well as a carriage to ride in.

By the time all this was finished the sun had gone down over Lough Erne and the stars were gleaming in the sky.

Phelim went to bed yawning but trying to pretend he wasn't a bit sleepy.

'Now it's your turn, Kathy!' said Mrs Clery.

'We'll need to be up early now there's a baby in the house.'

'You won't let the man take Jinny from us, will you, mammy?' pleaded Kathy.

Her mother shook her head.

'I don't think so,' she said. 'I couldn't bear to lose her now. If it hadn't been for this wee thing, I'd have been sitting here worrying about your father. Now I've a feeling he'll be as glad to have little Jinny as we are.'

Kathy folded her clothes on the chair beside her bed and said her prayers. She could hear her mother crooning to the baby:

> 'The stars look down
> And the wind glides by,
> Stirring the dust
> And the tree tops high.

Tapping the windows
And close-shut doors
Climbing the mountains
With baffled roars.
Sweeping the waves
And scattering the spray.
Seizing and tossing
The ungathered hay.

'Wearily singing
An old, old song.
It sighs and grieves
Over ancient wrong.
We in our cabin
Sleep and dream.
Drift in peace
On a quiet stream.
The door is closed
And the wind's away,
While we can rest
Till another day.'

THE EMPTY HOUSE

from *The Golden Caddy* (1962)

*The four children of the Fitzgerald family –
Gerry, Dina, Chris and Cathleen (known
as Kit) – are orphans, living in Dolmen
House, their Aunt Nono's home, in Co.
Clare. Their father has recently been killed
in a horse-riding accident and this means
that they may have to turn to their Uncle
Timothy Patrick, who lives in Cork, for
help. At first Gerry is against the idea, as he
does not like 'begging', but he knows they
have no choice. He and Dina leave the
warm, bright kitchen to fetch some paper
for Aunt Nono to write the letter to Uncle
Timothy Patrick.*

Now that Gerry was with her, Dina discovered
that the passage wasn't nearly so dark as she
expected. She could even see where it curved
round at the end of the staircase.

'Are you sure your exercise book is upstairs?'
asked Gerry, who was feeling lazy.

'I know it is! In the little cupboard, back of the
door in the children's room. I put it there
purposely with some other things.'

'Why?'

Dina stood thinking, her head on one side.

'I left them there so that I'd always have something to come back to if we had to go away.'

The boy gave her hair an affectionate little tug.

'You wouldn't want to come back to an empty house with only an exercise book to welcome you. Oh, Dina! You are a goose!'

They both laughed and ran to the end of the passage. There they stopped.

'How empty it looks!' sighed Dina.

She hadn't ventured into the front part of the house since that day she had stood at the foot of the big staircase watching the men carrying out a crate of china. When the door closed behind them she turned away, determined never to enter the hall again.

Yet here she was!

'Was it impossible to keep a resolution?' she wondered.

'Gerry,' she said softly. 'When you give your word to yourself to do something or not to do something, can you always keep your word?'

The boy frowned.

'I don't know! Sometimes I do, sometimes I don't. Does it matter?'

'It does!' declared Dina. 'I think it does. I'm sure it does!'

Gerry leaned against the wall.

'You can't always know what's going to happen.

I made up my mind never to leave Dolmen House. Yet, if Aunt Nono has her way, we'll most likely all be going off to Cork to live with strangers. What can I do about it? I don't want to leave Dolmen. I may have to. We'll all have to!'

'Just because we're children!' said Dina bitterly.

Gerry shook his head.

'Aunt Nono doesn't want to go any more than we do and she's not a child. Think of all the people we've known who emigrated. They went because they had to. They didn't want to go.'

'Some did!' said Dina indignantly. 'They went off laughing and singing. Didn't we see them, that day we were down at the crossroads?'

'You wouldn't have had them go away crying, would you?' asked Gerry reproachfully. 'They went bravely!'

'I know I'm a coward!' sighed the girl.

She tossed her head. A ray of pale sunshine wandering through a round window at the side of the great door turned her cloud of hair into a golden crown.

Gerry blinked. His sister was quite pretty. He hadn't noticed before.

'I've made up my mind,' declared Dina, 'once and for all. I'm not going to be a coward any more. In the future I'll be brave. I will! I will! You remind me if I forget, won't you?'

'You bet I will!' promised Gerry.

He grabbed her hand and they ran up the wide, carpetless stairs, their laughter rising before them.

When he flung open the end door on the fourth floor they stood silent.

Here was the room where they had spent so much of their young lives. The big square table which had occupied the centre of the floor was gone. Yet Gerry could see it – lesson books scattered at one end, toys, paint-boxes and Aunt Nono's sewing at the other.

He walked to the window and stood looking out at the drifting sleet now turning to snow.

From the window downstairs he was not able to see the wall where his father had been thrown. Now it stretched away to the right.

'How could I laugh?' he wondered, shocked at his own heartlessness. But Dina, who was the kindest, most affectionate girl in the world, had laughed too. He glanced over his shoulder.

'Dina! How could we laugh after what has happened?' he asked in wonder.

Dina did not answer. She stood with her back to him, her head inside the cupboard, her shoulders shaking as she tried to keep back her sobs.

He stood watching her unhappily. Suddenly Dina drew the back of her hand across her eyes.

'Daddy would be ashamed of me!' she exclaimed. 'I'll try not to cry again. It's so hard to be brave.'

'I'm just as bad as you are,' confessed Gerry. 'Only I'm crying inside. Let's find the exercise book and take it down. Aunt Nono will wonder what we're up to.'

He went over and stood there beside his sister, looking in at the deep shelves.

There had been one for each of them – Gerry's at the top, next Dina's, Chris and Kit's came last. The two bottom shelves and the big space beneath were filled with books, toys and games belonging to all four.

'Aunt Nono said we'd need them wherever we go. She said if we had our treasures we wouldn't feel so lonely,' murmured Dina.

'I'm too old for toys!' declared Gerry firmly.

'So am I!' said Dina. 'But not for books or games. I'd be terribly lonely without books.'

The boy nodded and took down one of his favourites, *Lost on Du-Corrig*. The cover was loose, the first and last pages missing.

'I haven't read that one,' Dina told him.

Gerry hesitated, then held it out.

'You can have it. I've read it heaps of times. Only, it's a boy's book.'

'I don't mind that,' she said. 'Often and often I like books I'm not supposed to like. Only, just lately I haven't read anything at all.'

'Remember, it's yours! Aunt Nono promised we could take all these when we go – if we have to leave. Hallo! Who's that?'

The heavy door was pushed slowly open and Kit appeared.

'Aunt Nono says are you lost? When are you coming down? She wants to write her letter.'

She came in, stared at the crowded shelves, shook her head as though bewildered by the jumble, then wandered over to the window. She looked as Gerry had done towards the wall at the far side of the stretch of smooth grass, put her hands over her eyes, turned and stumbled out into the passage.

'Poor little Kitten!' said Dina softly, using the old baby name for Kit. She ran after her sister.

Gerry sighed, took down the new exercise book from Dina's shelf and marched across the room.

He closed the door after him quietly, put his hand on the balustrade of the stairs as though he would jump on it and slide down as he used to do. But he drew his hand away and walked down the steps very sedately as if he were already grown up.

When he reached the kitchen the others were all seated watching the spatters of snow tapping at the pane.

His aunt smiled at him.

'Why don't you children sit round the fire. Maybe Dina could tell a story, or why wouldn't Gerry read one?'

Gerry knew she didn't want them to be

watching her while she wrote the letter.

'Come along, Dina!' he said. 'First, give me a hand to move the bench.'

The four of them carried this over to the fire and sat with their backs to Nono. Looking sideways they could watch the falling snow.

'It's too dark over here to read,' murmured Dina. 'We'll tell a story! Who will start?'

'You!' said her brothers and sister all together.

'I'll begin,' she agreed. 'When I'm tired, you can take turns.'

'Suppose we don't know it,' objected Chris.

'Make it up, of course, Silly!' and Kit gave him a dig with her elbow.

'I wish you'd get a bit fatter or stop digging!' he protested. 'Even if you are the youngest, you've no right to be poking holes in people!'

'What story shall I tell?' asked Dina quickly.

She knew which she would tell but she wanted to stop any chance of quarrelling.

'*The Snow Queen*,' answered Kit promptly, looking out at the snow which was falling quicker and more heavily each moment.

Gerry leaned back. He liked listening to Dina's story-telling, except when the story was a sad one. She found it so hard to keep herself from crying that it was difficult to understand a word she said.

Still the sad part of *The Snow Queen* didn't come at the beginning and he was sure Aunt Nono would have finished her letter by then, or she'd be demanding help.

'Go ahead!' he told Dina.

The younger ones nodded, Kit hugging herself.

Dina began:

'Once upon a time, there were two children who lived in a town across the sea. They were poor children and though they loved flowers, they hadn't the smallest garden between them, only a big wooden box on the window sill . . .'

Nono put down her pen and gazed thoughtfully at the group by the fire.

She wanted to make sure that she would do the very best for the children's happiness.

What would that be?

To stay here in the big empty house? No! That was impossible.

To rent the vacant cottage at the end of the village – the one they were always longing to live in and made up stories about?

Would they really be happy there, near the house where they had known so much joy? The House of Remembrance was its name in her mind.

Better go away, make a fresh start.

Suppose they were offered a home in Cork?

Her sister Kitty, she knew, hadn't liked many of her husband's relations. Would her children like them any more? Nono wondered.

'Sure, we're beggars, not choosers,' she

thought. 'We'll have to make the best of what's offered.'

'Suppose they offer to take the children but tell me to go my own way,' she mused. 'Whisha! I'm a fool to be meeting trouble half-way. Though how I'd live without the little rapscallions I don't know. I'd be fretting for fear they were lonesome or not well treated!'

'Still, I'm the one that would be lonesome if we're parted. I'd best start thinking about my own troubles.'

'Gerry!' she called. 'I've finished the letter. Would you fold it for me?'

'You're spoiling the story!' complained Kit.

She jumped up, ran over to her aunt and hugged her while Dina smiled thankfully.

'You won't go away from us, will you?' Kit whispered.

Nono shook her head.

'Not if I can help it!' she promised.

Gerry tore out the page Nono had filled with her small, neat handwriting, folded it in three and tucked in one end.

'Now you can write the address,' he told her.

She smiled at him and obeyed.

'Take it to the post, like a good lad,' she said. 'I wonder if you could take the list to the Stores as well. We need bread and eggs and anything Joe Coughlan will let us have. Ask for the bill. I may be able to pay him on Saturday.'

She tried to speak as if she had a bag filled with money. Gerry made a face and Dina turned away, trying to conceal how frightened she felt.

'Put on your macs and your big boots,' ordered Nono. 'Take your cap, Gerry, and you, Dina, pull up your hood. Run as hard as you can. Then you'll keep warm. Wait! I'll tuck the letter safely in your top pocket.'

'Do you want to go, Chris?' she asked.

The boy shook his head.

'I hate the cold!' he said. 'It's worse than an empty house.'

'So do I!' added Kit.

'Since when?' demanded Gerry jeeringly. 'You want Chris to read that book to you, I know. Only there's no beginning and no end!'

'Aunt Nono will make them up for us,' Kit assured him. 'And I'll tell you the whole story when you come back.'

'You haven't heard the end of *The Snow Queen* yet,' protested Dina.

Kit frowned.

'Oh dear! I'll be all mixed up. Never mind, Aunt Nono can tell us. You go along!'

She waved her hand and curled up in the middle of the seat, head turned to watch Gerry and Dina pulling on their macs, taking a market basket each, carefully opening the door a little way and slipping out.

A blast of bitter snow-laden wind whirled into the warm kitchen, then the door was closed and Nono joined the two by the fire.

'Tis a desperate day to send children out,' she sighed. 'I should have gone myself but I'd have to change into my boots, and they'll be twice as quick.'

'Gerry loves the wind,' Chris told his aunt comfortingly. 'So does Dina if he's with her.'

'The story!' Kit prompted. 'The story!'

REAL RELATIONS

from *The House by Lough Neagh* (1963)

Miles, Brede and Dara O'Donnell are orphans who live with their uncle and aunt on a farm at Carnduff, Co. Meath. When the farm has to be sold, the children are separated. Miles and Dara remain with the farm's new owner, while Brede (who is eleven) goes to Belfast with Cousin Martha, who owns a boarding house. However, things do not go very well for Brede in Belfast and she soon gets into trouble with Cousin Martha. She decides to run away to find her Uncle Colum and Auntie Bridgie, who have a farm near Lough Neagh, in Co. Antrim. But will they welcome her or send her away again, as Cousin Martha did?

Brede stared out through the window where the muslin curtains were swelling like sails. Beyond she saw the garden with its masses of flowers, farther still the fruit trees grew in orderly lines and away to the left the vegetable plots stretched side by side, with fowl houses and chicken runs, making a small town.

She looked at the table, still crowded with

plates, glasses, knives and forks – all the pleasant untidiness of dinner.

'I think I'd like even washing-up here!' Brede said slowly.

Her aunt laughed.

'You mustn't work today. There's a swing out yonder, hanging from the biggest apple tree in the orchard. You'll see all that's going on when you swing high. Best get acquainted today!'

'A swing!' cried Brede and jumping up she ran out of the house.

'This is a lovely place,' she thought. 'I wish Miles and Dara could come here. Maybe if I do everything I should, Aunt Bridgie and Uncle Colum will want the three of us. Then we *would* be happy!'

She found the swing. It had a wide seat, low down with thick ropes. At Carnduff the children tied a rope on a tree and used that. But this was wonderful – this was a real swing.

Slowly she pushed herself away from the ground and was soon flying through the air. Up and down! Up and down!

A light wind ruffled the leaves and showed the apples, the plums and pears clustered along the branches.

Brede had never seen such fruit. There were yellow apples, red ones, big green cookers. As for the plums – if she hadn't been so happy swinging through the warm air, she would have jumped off

and insisted on starting to pick them. She looked at the pears, ripe and inviting.

'I expect they'd let me eat some,' she said to herself. 'Of course I wouldn't eat a single one unless Aunt Bridgie told me I could. Anyway, I'd try not to!'

As she rose in the air she saw the great lake spreading out. There were sailing boats and rowing boats. She could hear a shout or two and for a moment envied the boys and girls who were helping to pull ropes, or dipping oars into the shining water.

'Wish I could be with them,' she thought.

She stopped the swing.

'I wouldn't be a bit surprised if one day I do learn to row, or maybe even swim. I'd love to go down into that water. It wouldn't be cold or dark. I know it wouldn't!'

Beyond the roofs and chimneys of the town she saw the turrets of the castle, and farther still the round tower.

Brede had never seen a round tower before, or a castle either. But she had seen pictures of them.

She gave a deep sigh. 'If only Miles and Dara were here in this lovely place, I'm almost sure that Dara would stop being bold. And even if he didn't, I believe they'd forgive him.'

Suddenly a big plum dropped into her lap. She closed her fingers over it and stared round.

She saw Uncle Colum standing up in a cart

holding on to the branch of a wide, spreading tree. On every branch there seemed to be as many plums as leaves. He was smiling at her.

She stood up and ran along by a green fence which separated the vegetables from the fruit trees.

'Thank you for the plum!' she called.

'Why don't you eat it?' he asked. 'Plums grow so that they'll be eaten. If you don't eat them the wasps will.'

'I don't like wasps!' declared Brede.

She remembered the wasps at Carnduff. Miles was sure they were the biggest, most spiteful wasps in the whole world. Yet they never stung him, though they were always stinging Dara.

'That's the first plum picked this season from our special plum tree,' Uncle Colum told her. 'Wish as you bite it!'

Brede plunged her teeth into the deep red fruit, juice spurted on to her face and the rich flavour made her eat it greedily. Yet she remembered to wish.

'Let Miles and Dara come here and go with me to the lake and the castle and the round tower!'

She let the sticky stone fall on the soft earth.

'Did you wish?' asked Uncle Colum.

Brede nodded.

'May it come true!' he said.

But he did not ask her what she wished. He knew that would be unlucky.

He pulled Brede up on the cart. Perched on the seat she could pick plums and put them into the big baskets standing side by side – or into her mouth.

'It's playing fair to eat every third one,' her uncle told her. 'More than that is cheating!'

His eyes danced and his face crinkled as he spoke. Brede soon understood why. The plums were so big and juicy that when she had eaten three she forgot to bite into another. The scent was all about her. The taste stayed on her tongue.

'You're a great little plum picker and a pretty good packer too,' Uncle Colum told her. 'You'll be a great help, only we mustn't let you work too hard.'

'Why not?' asked Brede. 'I love doing this.'

'Maybe you liked washing-up before you had too much of it,' he said, winking at her. 'Look what happened to Cousin Martha's crocks.'

They both laughed. Suddenly Brede became serious. 'I wish I hadn't,' she said. 'They were terrible grand. Cousin Martha will have to buy more and they'll cost a shocking amount of money. She told me so!'

'You couldn't help it,' Uncle Colum assured her.

'I could,' Brede said sadly. 'Cousin Martha told me not to pile them up. But I didn't want to keep going up and down stairs. You see, it really was my fault.'

Brede soon forgot Cousin Martha and her broken crocks. Every now and again she had to close her eyes and think of all that had happened since she last saw her cousin to make sure she wasn't dreaming. Yet when she opened her eyes she knew this was no dream.

Uncle Colum had stopped working. He was lighting his pipe and looking at her through a cloud of smoke he was puffing out.

'It's all real,' he told her. 'This won't fade away. From now on here is your home.'

'And I've real relations at last,' she said happily.

'Real relations!' he repeated, with a smile.

Brede felt more than ever that they were real relations when later on a letter came from Cousin Martha saying she never wanted to set eyes on Brede again.

'She is a clumsy, disobedient, ungrateful child,' wrote Cousin Martha, 'who did not appreciate the good home I gave her. If ye take her in, ye will only be asking for trouble, still, that is your affair!'

Brede opened her eyes wide as her uncle read the letter.

'You won't send me away, will you?' she pleaded, looking first at Aunt Bridgie, then at Uncle Colum.

'This is your home,' her aunt told her. 'You have nothing to be afraid of any more.'

And Uncle Colum nodded as hard as he could.

ALONE IN THE CAVE

from *Holiday at Rosquin* (1964)

Bernie Nagle, an orphan girl, lives with the Kelly family in Dublin. When the Kelly children decide not to spend their summer holidays in Rosquin with their cousins, the Dorans, she offers to go in their place. She soon becomes good friends with Garry Doran, who is confined to a wheelchair following an accident, and his friend Murty Pender. She, Garry and Murty enjoy many exciting adventures and the long summer days seem very short. Then a letter arrives from the Kellys, telling her that it is time to return to Dublin. But Bernie has come to love Rosquin, so she decides on a plan that will allow her to stay with her new friends, Garry and Murty.

Bernie hadn't been along this way since the day she and Garry had been carried by the current into the great cave when they were drifting in Joe Pender's small boat.

She looked down the slope, but there were no boats in the little harbour. She went on till she came to where the road turned sharply inland. A narrow track continued close to the cliff edge. She stopped there and looked about her.

'This must be where Garry had his accident,' she decided, peering cautiously over the edge.

'It's terribly slippy!' she murmured, moving back a little.

Some ten or twelve feet down a bare ledge of rock jutted out.

Bernie nodded solemnly.

'That's where Garry fell!' she repeated. 'I wonder how it really happened?'

The marks of the bicycle wheels had been wiped away by wind and rain.

'Garry needn't have come this far,' she continued. 'They were going up to the flower farm. If they had turned where they should he couldn't have fallen over the cliff, even if his bike had skidded. Oh, bother! It's beginning to rain.'

She went on, stepping very carefully, and suddenly she came to the entrance to the cave. A tall, slender rock, like a spear, rose before her. The path went round it a little way, then ended at a high narrow slit.

Bernie peeped inside. There was the cave. It was big and gloomy, except where the light from above showed jagged rocks looking like teeth in the mouth of some fierce giant.

'Oh!' she gasped, and shut her eyes. 'It's so big I'm frightened!'

The sound of rain on the rocks made her open her eyes.

'I'll just go inside,' she decided. 'At any rate I'll be dry in there!'

She stepped in and held her breath. When she was in the boat with Garry, Bernie hadn't paid a great deal of attention to her surroundings. She had been more concerned with the oars and the fear of being carried out to sea. Now she was thrilled by the beauty of the awe-inspiring spectacle.

Bernie had once been in Christ Church Cathedral in Dublin. Her cousin, Helen, had taken her there and Bernie had never forgotten the lofty arches and the beautiful music which rose till it seemed to pass beyond the roof into the sky. The cave reminded her of that experience.

'It's lovely but it scares me,' she thought. 'I do wish I had someone with me – Garry or Murty – anyone! Oh! What's that?'

She had been hearing a scraping, a whinny, a gruff voice growling – all mixed up – without understanding what she did hear. Now she looked up towards the opening she had entered by. A huge animal was standing there, crouched, showing its teeth in a ferocious grin.

Bernie trembled. Was it a lion? A tiger? It stood up as if ready to spring. She tried to move away noiselessly and found herself sliding, sliding, sliding.

She screamed and tried to stop. But she was on

a smooth stretch of rock where there was nothing for her to grip. Expecting a terrible bump she was even more startled when she landed on a soft heap of dry seaweed.

She screamed again when the fearsome animal leaped and came sliding down after her. Her scream changed to a tremulous laugh when she discovered her attacker was Murty's dog, Flipflap, who, dropping a crumpled handkerchief he held between his teeth, wriggled up close to her, licked her face and hands and tried to show that he had come to help her, not to attack her.

'Oh, Flipflap, you did frighten me,' she gasped, hugging him in relief.

Trying to push away a weight that had slipped down with her, she discovered the basket she had brought away from the kitchen. Nothing was harmed. The rug and her mac had saved even the bottle of lemonade.

Flipflap showed her what to do with the contents of the basket by seizing a packet of cream crackers and trying to tear away the paper wrapping.

Bernie snatched the packet. But, as a reward, she gave Flipflap a whole biscuit. They sat close together, crunching happily. The dog trotted over to where a thin stream of water trickled down the side of the cave and gulped at the drips.

'I'm thirsty too,' announced Bernie, unscrewing

the stopper of the lemonade bottle.

The bottle was big and heavy. Bernie carefully poured a little into her hand and sipped slowly. She screwed it up again and ate another biscuit. Flipflap came back to her and sat with his head on one side, his left ear poking straight up, his right ear down, the tip of his tongue just showing.

'I suppose you want another biscuit,' said Bernie.

Flipflap barked. He certainly did. The noise rose in a loud roar to the roof and he looked as startled as Bernie.

'We must keep very quiet,' she whispered. 'Don't you know I'm hiding? If you keep on making such a shocking noise I'll be discovered before I want to be. Then I'll have to go back to Dublin and maybe you'll never see me again.'

Tears filled her eyes at the prospect and she sniffed.

Flipflap flung himself at her and licked her face wildly. His wet, soft tongue felt very comforting and she began to smile.

'I'm lucky to have you here,' she told him. 'I'd soon feel lonesome if I were alone. But I do wish you had brought Murty with you.'

Flipflap sighed, stretched himself out and went to sleep.

'If only I had a storybook,' murmured Bernie.

Keeping very still so that she would not disturb

her companion, Bernie looked about her.

'I'm lucky to have this lovely bed of seaweed,' she said. 'Only I don't like the smell much. I'll pretend I'm on a desert island and I'll arrange my things. I'll put my rug where I can pull it over me when I'm going to sleep. The mac can go on top. Now I'll unpack the basket!'

As well as the cream crackers she had a packet of Golden Grain biscuits, one of Rice Crispies and a bunch of bananas. One of these was a little soft. She ate this at once so that it wouldn't spoil. There were a few slices of ham, a packet of cheese, a bag of fresh soft rolls, a large soda cake and half a pound of butter.

'I wonder how many days I'll have to stay here?' she thought. 'Maybe I needn't stay very long. Oo! What's this?'

It was Mrs Pender's library book which she had poked in the grocery basket without thinking. Mrs Pender was even now back in her cottage trying to find it, but Bernie wasn't thinking of her. She was delighted at having the chance of reading, reading without having to do anything else until the book was finished.

She looked at the cover and read the title – *Uncle Tom's Cabin*.

Bernie hugged herself.

'I love stories about cabins,' she told Flipflap. 'I've always wanted to live in one on the side of a mountain, just above the sea – one with a thatched roof and whitewashed walls. If you're a good dog I'll read this to you – some of it, not all! It's a big book, you know, and maybe I won't have to stay here very long. I wonder how long I should stay?'

She propped herself against a rock where a shaft of sunlight gave light and warmth, and began to read the first page.

THE LITTLE FIDDLER

from *The Twisted Key
and Other Stories* (1964)

*Fintan Shanahan is a fiddler who knows
every kind of tune that can be fiddled. He
plays his fiddle on the street for the crowds
of shoppers who sometimes reward him by
throwing a few coppers into his cap. Fintan
must play every fiddling tune he knows to
make enough money to buy food for himself
and his dog, Spats. One day Fintan and
Spats are joined by a strange new
companion and don't quite know what to
make of him.*

F intan Shanahan sat on a high stone step in an
arched doorway at the corner of the Coal Quay
in Cork City. He had chosen a spot where he was
well sheltered from the bitter wind which blew
along the River Lee.

Beside him stretched out Spats, his dog,
elegant with his thick, black coat and white paws,
who was anxiously watching the parcel wrapped in
newspaper which rested on Fintan's knees. At the
other side of the step lay Fintan's fiddle, snug in its
thick bag.

'I'm famished wid the cold,' said Fintan the
fiddler. 'I'm tired too, for there's nothing harder
than playing to a crowd that's doing the last bit of
buying for the weekend and meeting friends.
They're too busy to spare a minit listening to the
tunes of their native land.'

Spats whined impatiently and put a paw on his
master's knee. He looked at Fintan, one ear up, the
other down, and thumped the step with his stumpy
tail.

Fintan smiled and unwrapped the parcel.

'Cheese sandwiches!' he said. 'Fresh soda-bread
baked in the old, iron hot oven, creamy cheese, not
to mind the thick spreading of good farmers'
butter. Ye shall have yer share! And to-morra, if I've
earned the price of a decent dinner before we go
home, ye'll have all the bones and pieces ye can
manage.'

He broke off a thick piece of crust. Spats lifted
his head and bit into it eagerly. Fintan was about to
eat some of the softer bread when he stopped and
stared.

Almost as close to him as Spats, stood the
queerest little fellow he had ever set eyes on. The
archway was dark so he couldn't make out whether
the stranger was a boy or a little man who was
gazing hungrily at the sandwich.

'Decently dressed and well shod, yet there's a
hungry look about him,' muttered the fiddler.

'Have a bite,' he offered. 'You're very welcome.'

The little fellow reached out, grabbed the bread and cheese and crammed it into his mouth.

'God help us!' thought Fintan. 'There's no manners about nowadays. But, sure, the poor scrap must be starving!'

He took up a second sandwich.

The tiny hand, red with cold, snatched it from him.

Spats growled.

''Pon me word –!' began Fintan indignantly, then checked himself. 'What kind of a savage am I to grudge a child a share of me food?'

He held out a third sandwich. To his surprise the stranger held back and looked at the fiddler with his head on one side.

'Ye're too generous,' he mumbled. ''Tis a cold day and ye need the good food yerself.'

'The decent little chap!' thought Fintan.

'Take it and welcome,' he said. 'Wouldn't it be strange if we couldn't share with one another once in a while?'

'Thank ye kindly,' said the other, settling himself on the step beside Fintan and laying down the long bundle he had under his arm.

Spats gave a growl.

'Quiet!' ordered Fintan. 'Would ye growl at a guest? Have ye no manners at all?'

'Is that a fiddle ye have?' asked Fintan, looking

curiously at the stranger's bundle, for he caught sight of the polished wood and gleaming strings.

'What else would it be?' snapped the other.

'You don't come from these parts, do ye? What name is on ye?' asked Fintan. 'I never set eyes on ye before, and I do be playing round and about most of the time.'

'I do not come from these parts,' was the answer. 'My name is Cleary.'

'No offence intended,' said Fintan. 'That looks a good fiddle, what I can see of it. But a trifle on the small side. When I was young they thought I had the gift, but I'd little chance to learn for I had to earn me living. Yet I loved the fiddle, and when all else failed I went back to it. What's yer favourite piece?'

'*The Secret Land*,' answered Cleary, with a grin.

Fintan wrinkled up his face.

'I never heard that one. I wonder now, would ye mind playing the tune? I mean – if ye know it well enough?'

The stranger's eyes flashed.

'Me not to know any tune in the wide world!' he cried indignantly.

'Sure, I meant no harm.'

Fintan was apologising when a crowd of ragged boys came racing along the quays. Snatching up the fiddle, Cleary darted off. The boys gathered round Fintan.

'Hi, Mister Shanahan, play us a piece, will ye?' cried the leader, a wild-looking lad with red tousled hair and tattered clothes.

'I will, then!' agreed Fintan.

This was not the audience he had been longing for – one that would fill his old caubeen of a hat with enough money to buy tomorrow's dinner and a trifle over. But he liked children.

'What shall I play?' he asked. 'It must be one tune only.'

'*O'Donnell Abu*,' cried one.

'*Out and Make Way*,' shouted another.

Fintan laughed.

'Ye're good patriots, that's sure! What about *The Harp that Once*?'

'Anything ye say, mister! Anything at all!' said the red-haired lad.

The other nodded.

Fintan put down his hand and lifted the fiddle.

The moment his fingers touched it he knew it wasn't *his* fiddle but the stranger's.

'Ah, well, he'll be back for it when he learns his mistake,' thought Fintan. 'Whisha! Tis desprit small!'

He tucked it under his chin and drew the bow across the strings.

He meant to play *The Harp that Once*, but the melody which came from the strings was strange to him. His fingers held the bow but it seemed that other fingers were guiding it. He listened as if in a dream, not seeing that the crowd before him was growing larger every moment.

'That fiddler shouldn't be playing in the streets!' said an indignant voice. 'He should be heard in the biggest halls all over Ireland!'

'Shh-shh!' ordered another. 'We'll never get the chance to hear such music again.'

Then Fintan caught sight of the real owner of the fiddle coming back. He carried the big fiddle over his shoulder as if it were a great weight. As he reached the crowd he stopped and stood listening.

Fintan ceased playing.

'That's all for today!' he said. 'How about a hansel for the musician? Here, lad! Take the old caubeen!'

He put his hat down, gave the red-headed boy a slap on the shoulder, and slipped round the side of the crowd.

Cleary stood there smiling cheerfully.

'Here's yer property back, little brother of the bow,' Fintan said. 'Ye made a mistake and did me a good turn.'

'Ye have the touch,' said the small fiddler. 'That's why you could play our own tune – *The Secret Land*. You shared your feed with me. I'll share what magic I have with you.'

They exchanged fiddles, and when Fintan held his own shabby instrument he felt an old friend

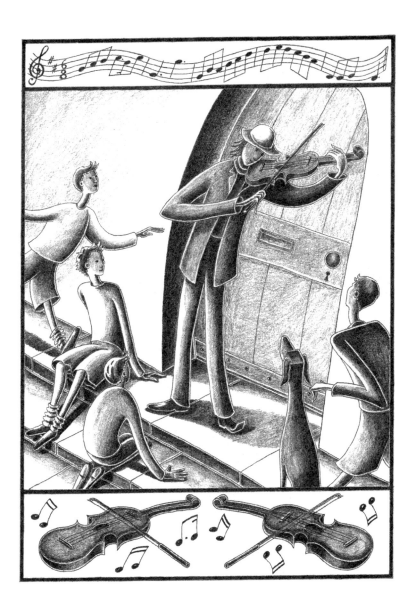

had come back to him.

He turned to thank Cleary but he was alone. He went back to the step. The crowd had gone. The boy and Spats sat side by side; the hat, filled to the brim with coins, lay before them.

'We're taking care of the money, Mister Shanahan,' said the boy. 'Can I help ye carry it home?'

'We'll find something better to carry it in,' said the fiddler. 'I don't want me best hat to be destroyed on me altogether.'

He drew a canvas bag from his pocket. It had never been full before. Now there was enough even to make a pleasant jingle in his pocket, besides a handful for the boy.

'Ye've earned that,' said Fintan. 'Now I'll play one last tune.'

He stood there in the gathering darkness, with the lights coming out along the frosty quays and glittering up on the hills above Cork and, drawing his bow across the strings, he played *The Secret Land*.

GLOSSARY

Chapter 2: The Cabin in the Mountains
Creepy: a small stool, usually with three legs
Avic: son (in Irish, *a mhic*: oh, my son)
Higgler: a person who buys and sells goods

Chapter 3: Four White Swans
Sorra one o' me knows: I really do not have any idea
Fine atin: food which is delicious to eat
Crathures: creatures, beings
Ere: ever, possibly
Bedad: by God!
Quare: strange
Allanna: child (in Irish, *a leanbh*: oh, my child)
Right here forninst ye: directly in front of you

Chapter 5: Sky Farm
An a dale too cocked up in the sky for me likin: and a bit too high up as far as I'm concerned
Manes: means
Bonaveens: piglets
Erra: ever
Dure: door
Slane: type of spade used for cutting peat

Chapter 6: The Shadow Pedlar
Settle: a long high-backed bench
Bonhams: piglets
Tammy: a cap with a broad circular flat top

Lave us stow: allow us to put

Chapter 7: The Fairy Fort of Sheen
Colloughing: chatting, talking confidentially

Chapter 9: If I Were a Blackbird
Piece: food brought to school to eat
Gerrul: girl

Chapter 10: The Liverpool Boat
Raisin: reason

Chapter 13: Real Relations
Crocks: dishes, cups, saucers and plates

Chapter 15: The Little Fiddler
Caubeen: a man's woollen hat
Hansel: a good luck gift

Also by Robert Dunbar

ENCHANTED JOURNEYS

FIFTY YEARS OF IRISH WRITING FOR CHILDREN

In this anthology, a beautiful companion volume to
Secret Lands, Robert Dunbar gathers together excerpts
from the work of some of Ireland's finest writers. Span-
ning the last fifty years of literature for children, these
stories combine adventure, danger, intrigue and mys-
tery with evocative images of an ever-changing Ireland.
Enchanted Journeys includes the work of Marita
Conlon-McKenna, Frank Murphy, Maeve Friel, Tom
McCaughren, Elizabeth O'Hara, Sam McBratney,
Siobhán Parkinson, Matthew Sweeney, Martin Waddell,
John Quinn, Eugene McCabe, Janet McNeill, Meta
Mayne Reid, Walter Macken, Patricia Lynch, Eilís Dillon
and Conor O'Brien.

Send for our full colour catalogue